NUMBER SEVEN AND THE LIFE LEFT BEHIND

Number Seven and the Life Left Behind

HIRTZEL

Contents

Copyright x

Dedication xi

1   1

2   10

3   26

4   35

5   50

6   68

7   78

8   83

9   94

10   110

11   130

0   139

About the Author 152

ACKNOWLEDGMENTS

No story comes to realization in a vacuum. I am grateful to all my writer and reader friends who have continued to support me on my journey, but specific thanks are due to the following:

Sue, who awakened in me the initial glimmerings of Seven's story;

Tricia, who reined in all of my happy commas with expertise and without complaint;

Ken, whose invitation to the Amorphous Publishing Guild allowed this publication to happen on my own terms;

Chase, who graciously gave Seven his first chance to entertain and whose first feedback was invaluable to the final story;

and *Seth*, who listened, read, and let the story be what it is, and me who I am.

Chapter 1

NUMBER SEVEN KNEW from the moment they met that guarding young Kirill Morozov would be the last job he'd ever do. Not because the young Olympic hopeful was a snooty, demanding, or difficult assignment. In fact, quite the opposite. It was hard not to like him even when he was being obnoxious, as was the case tonight.

"Look!" Kirill demanded. Three years together had made them colloquial and comradely, to the point where the string of lewd messages sent from his team-mates neither embarrassed nor deterred him from shoving the phone into Seven's face. "Even Darya is there."

Among the dim, blurry photos of loose-limbed young ladies, Seven recognized the blonde stunner with the whipping ponytail. Like Kirill, she stood out from a crowd as much by presence as by beauty. Nevertheless, Seven leaned away. "So she is."

Kirill took his phone back, holding it in both hands with the same reverence one might show a gold medal. "She is fantastic," he wheezed. "Did you know she can do an armstand back double-somersault with one-and-a-half twists, and barely break the water going in?"

Seven knew what that mishmash of words meant, and the impressiveness implied. It didn't compare to Kirill's time for the 200m butterfly, though, which put him well on his way to becoming a world record-holder. Seven hunched one shoulder up. "If you like that sort of thing."

"What's not to like?" Kirill said, still ogling. He finally pulled his gaze away and looked up at Seven with once-more-brilliant eyes. "Can we go? Please, say we can go."

Seven held back a sad smile. Getting permission from his superiors at the security division to take Kirill off the grounds on a standard training night was difficult enough. To do so just for the sake of a party in the city, which was a forty-five-minute drive in the best of traffic, was pushing insubordination. But Seven touched the communications bud in his ear to make sure the vibration mic was activated and made the effort anyway.

"Control?" he said. "Requesting permission to—"

"Request denied, Number Seven." The voice on the other end was clipped, stoic, and female without being feminine. "You are to escort your charge to his room and secure him for the night. And, make sure he has his supplements."

Seven glanced at Kirill, who'd clasped his hands in a tight-fingered prayer gesture and was grimacing a silent, drawn-out *Please?* He turned his head away, muttering, "It is just a party. I don't see why—"

"Yours is not to question why," the voice at Control told him. "Yours is to follow orders. And Number Two has given his orders. Control, out." In his ear, the faint whistle of connection went dead with a click.

Seven stood straight and turned to Kirill with a ready look of apology. "The old man says no."

"That's not fair!" Kirill complained. The woman on duty behind the reception desk cast them a snooping glance but returned to her computer screen when Seven met her gaze. He had that effect on people.

"Please," Kirill begged. "Ask again?"

"It would not do any good." Once division command came down with a decision, that decision was done.

Seven walked over to the bank of lifts, leaving Kirill to follow. He pressed the call button and tried to be reasonable. "They will probably break it up before we could get there, anyway. You know how Two likes to throw his weight around."

Beside him, Kirill's baritone swung into a grumble. "No one even told me they were going to a party. I wouldn't have gone back to the pool, if I'd known."

"Your training is important," Seven began when Kirill groaned, loudly and long enough to deflate his posture.

"I'm always in training! I swim faster and stronger than anyone on our team or any other. But every day, it's the same thing: 'You need to be ready for trials,'" he said, affecting a sneer and a mimic of his coach's deeper, lazy basso. "'You need to be better for Masters. The Olympic committee doesn't like losers.'" He returned his voice to normal for another grumble. "Meanwhile, Ullman and Adamski and everyone else get to go out and get laid as much as they want."

"Adamski is a clown," Seven said without looking his way. "And Ullman is an ass. No woman in their right mind would give either of them the time of day, let alone anything else."

"They still get to go!"

The lift dinged and the doors came open. Kirill loped inside, moving to the back to rest against the bar. Seven went in after him and pushed the button for their floor. The low chime of the rising floors was the only thing to break the quiet, until Seven turned to Kirill with more sympathy.

"I understand how you feel," he said, but the swimmer humphed.

"No, you don't."

Seven held back a harrumph of his own. "You are not the only young man ever to be told he cannot have something he wants."

Kirill's stare stayed on his sneakers. "Just the only one who will die never having made love to a beautiful woman," he muttered.

On the other side of the car, Seven snorted. "Stop being dramatic."

"I'm not being dramatic!" Kirill straightened all the way up. He wasn't as buff or as tall as Seven, but he was built in that classically handsome, heroic swimmer's image, and very nearly capable at his full six-foot height to look Seven in his good eye. "Even the women here don't notice me. I say hello to them every day, and every time, they walk right by me like I am not even there."

"I have seen you say hello," Seven said, and glowered at him. "...to their busts and behinds. Did you ever stop to think that their ignoring you has something to do with that?"

Kirill bit his lips closed for a second of shamed self-awareness. Seven let him fret in silence. When the lift opened on their floor, Kirill attempted a weak excuse.

"I can't help it if those are their most interesting features."

"Sometimes, I despair of you," Seven mumbled, and nodded to the doors.

Kirill walked out, spreading his long arms in a clueless, *can-you-blame-me?* gesture. "What?"

"A woman is more than the sum of her measurements," Seven told him as he kept stride. "They are minds, and hearts, and strength, and—"

"I know that." Kirill stopped in front of the door to the suite. "But how am I supposed to get to know any woman when I am training, training, training all of the time? I want to *live*."

Seven pulled the suite's key card from inside his jacket and tapped it to the security pad. "You live very well." To prove his point, he pushed the door open and flipped on the entrance light, illuminating the suite's luxury of size and aspect; only Number Two had larger quarters, what used to be the Presidential Suite on the top floor. This one was still the most lavish accommodation for anyone who wasn't the security division's overseer in the field, though, with two private bedrooms with baths, a fully equipped kitchenette, an entertainment center across from the lush sectional sofa, and a work space facing the windows.

Kirill walked in around him and went straight to the sofa, seemingly oblivious to it all. "Hotel rooms," he griped. "Pools. Gymnasiums. It's *boring*!"

Seven had hung back in the entrance hall to put his suit jacket in the closet, but now crossed his arms over his wide chest. "Many people would be very happy with boring. I would have been, at your age."

"I know swimming is not soldiering," Kirill said, briefly cowed before he rebounded again. "But at least you had your freedom! You saw the world. You must have had tons of women!"

"I also got this," Seven said, indicating his face and its harsh reality.

"The scar is cool," Kirill muttered behind a snort. "Everybody thinks so."

"You think it is cool to get shot at? To spend your nights shivering under a desert sky, wondering if you are going to make it home alive or in a casket, or at all? Because that is what my life was like." Seven waved his hands around. "I did not have my own suite in a four-star hotel, with my choice of waffles with strawberries or custom-made omelettes for breakfast, or a personal massage instead of the group sauna."

Kirill's gaze flicked away. "You are saying I'm spoiled and ungrateful."

A swell of guilt pulled down Seven's mouth. He drew a deep breath and let it go, more to settle himself than to convince Kirill, and approached the sofa. He put his hand on Kirill's firm shoulder and gave it a quick squeeze, in what he hoped would be taken as assurance.

"I am saying that everyone has crosses to bear. You are right," Seven said. "You are the best swimmer on this team or any other. Which means you are held to a higher standard than everyone else." He tried a comforting smile. "Your time will come."

Kirill looked at him a long time, not moving or speaking. Seven could tell his words had reached him, though; the lack of another outburst was proof of that.

At last, Kirill sighed and pushed himself to his feet. "It's already been twenty-two years." He spread his arms in a gesture of acceptance. "What is one more night, eh?" he said, and headed for his bedroom.

Seven shifted into his place on the sofa and watched him go. Like the rest of the athletes at the compound, Kirill possessed a deep-seated drive to succeed. He also had the impatience that came with that trait. But he was thoughtful, too, in his sheltered young man's way, and very agreeable; his demands had never gone beyond wanting a second bowl of ice cream at dinner or asking for some extra time in the sauna. He was due for a bit of wish-fulfilment, though Seven wasn't sure how. Parties weren't his strong suit, and he didn't really know anyone outside of his job.

He picked up the remote control for the television and switched it on. It landed on the news, in the middle of a report about the latest border arrests of desperate immigrants trying to enter and the disillusioned marginalized trying to escape, complete with video footage of men and women in military armor threatening a line of protesters with their weapons and shields.

Seven grimaced at the screen. He sympathized with the military's day-to-day actors just following orders, but turning aside or locking away people simply because they didn't fit the administration's idea of the preferred citizen? That wasn't what he'd fought and bled for. Someone in the ranks had to stand up against the injustices, soon. It was, after all, often easier to ask for forgiveness than ask for permission.

Seven paused. It had been Natalya to tell him that all those years ago, when he'd run from the boys' home to the army recruitment center in an effort to get out of a life destined for defeat.

He pulled his phone from his pocket and scrolled through the contacts list. He tapped the dial icon with his thumb, pulled the comm from his ear to keep this conversation private, and waited for an answer.

Three rings went by before a feminine voice as rich and smooth as chocolate truffles said, "Allo?"

"Natalya!" He couldn't quite keep a smile from blooming. "Long time no talk, eh?"

"Who is this?"

"Your favorite ex-war hero."

"You'll have to be more specific."

He frowned. "Quit fooling. You know it's me."

Her voice broke suddenly, into a laugh of sharp delight. "My darling sourpuss! Still so easy to tease."

"Still so eager to do so."

A pause before her tone took on a leading lilt. "It's been a while."

He nodded against the phone. "I know."

She didn't dwell on their time without talking. "To what do I owe this unexpected pleasure?"

His smile returned. "Are you still in the entertainment business?"

"It's the most honest way for an enterprising woman to make a living," she said with a blasé straightforwardness; he imagined her glancing at her nails as she spoke. "Why do you ask?"

Seven looked at Kirill's bedroom door. Beyond, he could hear the shower running. He snickered. "How would you like me to owe you a favor?"

Chapter 2

STANDING OUTSIDE THE pool showers in his suit, Seven sweltered. Of course, the training complex had other places he could have waited, but Seven preferred staying close to his charge. So when Kirill hobbled out from his shower naked and dripping, Seven was there, ready with a towel and some praise.

"That was one of your best times."

Kirill smiled, and rubbed the towel once over his head before cinching it around his waist. "You watched me?"

"That is my job." Seven followed him over to the lockers but stopped him before Kirill pulled out his usual post-training wear.

"No jeans and hoodie," Seven said, and opened the next locker over, which was usually empty; the team members were few enough, even with the women's team included, to keep several unclaimed locker spaces between them. This time, though, Seven had prepped the locker with a long garment bag, which he drew out with a little shake. "You need to look nice tonight."

Kirill blinked. "Why?"

"We are meeting someone."

"Who?"

A smile pulled at one side of Seven's mouth. "Someone with an impressive sum of measurements."

Kirill's eyes went wide, then flashed with sudden excitement. He threw his arms around Seven, exclaiming in a kind of half-shout and half-squeal, "You are the best!"

Seven laughed and eased him away. "And you are wet."

Kirill surrendered to a brief blush and stepped back. He unwrapped his towel for a pat-down, and, looking up between swipes of his long, muscled legs, asked, "What is she like?"

"Her name is Natalya," Seven said, turning his gaze to the more mundane sight of the circulation vents near the ceiling. "And she is..." He tipped his head back and forth, hunting for a diplomatic description before settling on, "...an independent businesswoman."

He heard Kirill chortle. "You are such a gentleman!"

"As you should be." Seven fixed him with a stern and pointed look, regardless of his state of undress. "Just because this is her job does not mean she is undeserving of your full respect. Do you understand?"

Kirill paused at this chastising, in the middle of putting on his long-sleeved button-down. He pulled his lips together and bobbed his head.

"Good," Seven said, and let the stumble go. "Natalya is a shrewd and worldly woman, but she is also a friend. I trust her, and so can you."

Kirill stayed still, save for an inquisitive tilt of his head. "Is she pretty?" he asked in a tentative voice.

Seven left him to agonize a moment before breaking into another smile. "A knockout," he said, and Kirill grinned and nearly bounced out of his skin.

He kept bouncing as he dressed, then bounced all the way to the car, the entire drive into the city, even as they walked up to the drab gray apartment tower over-looking the park. There Seven stopped him with a hand on his shoulder.

"As far as anyone else is concerned," he said, lowering his chin to keep his tone hushed, "we are out in the city, getting something to eat."

"Something delicious!" Kirill said, but Seven glared.

"Be serious."

Kirill sobered. "Sorry." He glanced down at himself and back up to Seven again. "How do I look?"

Seven stepped in to straighten Kirill's tie, which had skewed to the left from his fidgeting. "Very handsome," he said truthfully, as he finished fixing the placement of the knot. "Now," he went on, "Natalya may ask you if you want to do things, and that is your choice to say yes or no. But you do not take her choice for granted. Which means that you do not assume, with your mouth or your hands or...any other part of you."

Kirill's eyes went abruptly wide. "What kind of things?"

"Things you do not go bragging about afterward to your friends," Seven said, holding in a smile for the younger man's naivety.

Kirill shrugged. "You are my only friend."

Seven pressed the ringer for Natalya's apartment and looked into the security camera lens. "So, don't tell me."

The panel speaker crackled, and Natalya's voice said, "Is that a one-eyed devil come knocking at my door?"

Seven cringed in mild embarrassment. "Will you let us in, or do I need to huff and puff?"

The door buzzed, and Seven ushered Kirill through. They took the lift up to the sixth floor and walked down the hall to Natalya's apartment, where Seven rapped on the door. It opened, and the scent of white jasmine tickled Seven's nose before he even saw her.

She was very much the same woman he remembered. Older, of course, and a bit thinner in the face, but still straight-backed and statuesque; still with the bust and behind that defied gravity; still with the bright green eyes and high cheekbones that, together with her lustrous black hair, gave the impression of a panther on the prowl.

"Ah!" She sized up Kirill with her feline smile. "You've brought me a prince, I see."

Kirill had frozen suddenly dumb, his gaze glued to Natalya's form-fitting dress with its decorated bodice and thigh-high slit. Seven nudged him, causing him to blurt:

"Uh! It's...a pleasure to meet you. I am Kirill."

"Kirill," Natalya repeated, and shot Seven a smirk. "It is my pleasure, too. Come in, please."

She led them through the door and into the apartment. They passed through the small open kitchen to the large living area, where she stopped, turned, and said, "Would you like a drink?"

"He doesn't need a drink," Seven said, but Natalya snorted.

"I think I know better than you what our young prince needs. Just a little something to help you relax," she said, stroking a long finger over Kirill's cheek; Seven noticed each nail had a slightly different swirl pattern painted across it. "I have vodka, whisky, beer...?"

Kirill swallowed, and blinked for what seemed like the first time in a full minute. "Uh, a beer would be nice. Thank you."

"Nothing too strong," Seven said.

Natalya's smile slacked a bit at his warning. "Do I have to put you outside?" She turned her winsome expression back to Kirill. "Shall we put him outside, like the annoying dog he's being?"

His sense of responsibility, loyalty, or some other reluctance caused Kirill to falter for an answer. In the pause, Seven made an offer.

"Let me have some of that whisky you mentioned, and I'll shut up and watch the television. Okay?"

That seemed to satisfy her. "There are tumblers in the bar," she said, pointing to a shallow shelf and mini-refrigerator beneath the living room window. She slipped her arm through Kirill's and put out her other arm, giving a blind waggle of her fingers. "And, hand me a beer. We'll share it inside," she said, holding Kirill's stupidly mesmerized gaze.

Seven went to the bar, popped a cold beer from the refrigerator, and put it in her hand. "Be gentle," he said to Natalya, because Kirill wasn't paying attention to him.

Natalya didn't take her eyes from the younger man but said, "Don't worry. He is in good hands." She drew Kirill toward the bedroom door, beyond the threshold of which Seven could see an impressively large and well-laid-out bed. "Come, sweet prince. We will get to know each other better, away from these distractions."

Seven got a glimpse of Kirill's eagerly flushed face before Natalya pulled him into both the bedroom and a close embrace. Then she closed the door, leaving Seven alone.

He went back to the bar and poured himself a whisky – a fine, forty-year-old Highland Park with a pleasant burn in the nose – and took a more discerning glance around the apartment. It was not as large as the suite he shared with Kirill back at the hotel, but it was decorated well, and at fair expense. The kitchen appeared functional and modern, with a few high-end appliances perched pristinely on the counter. Gifts, perhaps, because in all the years he'd known her, Natalya had only ever been able to cook coffee. The living room, predictably, felt more lived-in, with the mahogany bar, a loveseat and chaise in matching russet, and a small table with a manicured spread of attractive books that had probably never even been opened.

He took a sip of the whisky and sat down on the loveseat to turn on the television. He kept the volume low so as not to disturb the next room...but also to stay aware if he might be needed, just in case.

The television came on to one of those comprehensive news shows, where a blandly benign talking head rattled off a report of plummeting stock averages, mounting guerrilla terrorist strikes, and militarized deportations, all with a pitch and intonation practiced to the point of being indistinguishable from any ratings rival. He was replaced by a feminine doppelganger who beamed a too-white smile for a story about the same-day births of two new celebrity babies, one born to a former Olympic figure skater and her tech-giant entrepreneur husband, the other to some big banking CEO and her track-and-field star husband who had graciously taken a break from his rigorous training schedule to pose for the press. The newscasters expounded for a few minutes about how beautiful the babies and their parents were, especially the athletes, to the point where Seven had to change the channel. The satellite frequency scan took a moment, though, and in that brief silence, he heard Kirill wheeze a noise of reedy delight.

Seven chased his grimace with a gulp of his whisky and upped the volume on the television.

He found a banal but pretty mystery show and settled back into the cushions, concentrating more on the details of the tropical scenery than the drama; he had enough of that to deal with in his real life. At some point, he dozed off on the loveseat to the soporific storyline.

He came to with a sharp snort, as someone poked his arm.

"Some bodyguard you are," Natalya muttered. She clinked his glass with the lip of the bottle.

"No, no." He waved her away and struggled to sit up. "I have to drive."

"Then I'll drink it." She took his glass and swigged, ending with a shimmy of her shoulders. She'd replaced her dress with a dressing gown in red silk stitched with black lace flowers along the edges and let down her hair into a shiny onyx cascade that made her look much more like the Natalya he used to know. Her long sigh as she finished her drink sounded like the old Natalya, too, and he smiled.

"It is good to see you again," he said in a hushed voice, as she let the glass come down and looked at him. "I did not realize, until tonight...." He paused on the sentiment hovering at the tip of his tongue.

She waved her long lashes in a slow blink. "What?"

"How much I have missed you."

"I've always been here," she said, gently scolding.

"I know." He glanced away, to his feet. "But...!"

"I know," she echoed, and drew a breath that came out not-quite-sigh and not-quite-scoff. "Your traditional Ukrainian devotion to the job."

He nodded, feeling a little bit of shame but mostly resignation. "Speaking of," he said, to change the subject from the reason he'd let their friendship lapse. "How did he do?"

Her dressing gown slipped open to her thighs as she crossed her legs and relaxed against the cushions. "A bit bumpy, to start. But sweet." Her naked lips curled into a smile touched with devilish mischief. "And, *very* receptive to suggestion, if you know what I mean."

Seven raised his hand and made a face. "Please, do not tell me."

Natalya let out a trilling laugh. "Oh! Is the big, bad soldier suddenly squeamish?"

"I am not squeamish," he corrected over her lingering laughter. "I simply believe that what a man does behind closed doors is no one's business but his own."

"And the person he is with," she said with a leading smirk.

"If there is one."

She pushed out her bottom lip to its fullest, in an exaggerated pout that made him chuckle. "Poor you. Would you like me to help?"

"No," he said, too quickly. Then: "Thank you."

"I did not mean services," she said, guessing at his reason for refusal. "I know lots of people. Lonely souls just looking for companionship."

"I'm certain you do." He smiled for her. "But, I am fine."

"No, you're not." She leaned close; he felt the weight of her breasts against his arm. "How long has it been for you?"

He cracked a snicker. "About seven inches."

She eased away with a click of her tongue and a roll of her eyes. "You're so concerned with protecting others, you don't take the time to look after yourself. But it's not too late, you know. You are still young."

"You think thirty-six is young?" he asked, still teasing.

She glowered and challenged him, "You think thirty-four is old?"

He raised both hands in a gesture of surrender. "No, no! You are still very beautiful."

She relaxed with a sigh. "And you are still very handsome."

In her eyes, he saw a subtle sadness. Before he could offer her any reassurance, though, Kirill said from behind them:

"I keep telling him that. But he is all about the job."

"That job is you," Seven reminded, and turned to look back at him. While the swimmer had redressed into his slim-cut shirt and trousers, he seemed to wear them with a different air. He walked with a smoother sway, too, and smiled in a way that brought the word languorous to mind.

"My prince!" Natalya swept up to meet him, her robe twirling around her legs like a ballroom dancer's. "You are leaving already?"

Kirill accepted the wind of her arms, bowing his head as a kind of bashful excuse. "I have to get up early, for training."

"Then train," Natalya said, pressing her body against his with the poise of a true professional. "And win." She smiled a white, flattering smile, adding, "For me," just before she drew his face to hers for a kiss that was long if not deep.

Seven got to his feet. "All right, Romeo," he began, but Natalya brushed him off.

"Romeo is a boy," she said, caressing Kirill's cheek. "This one is a *man*. Like Marc Antony."

Seven humored her with a tight smile. "You just want to be Cleopatra." He put a hand on Kirill's shoulder. "Come on. We need to be back before Two makes his rounds."

"I have to go," Kirill told Natalya. "But, thank you." He paused to make a fresh smile. "My queen."

Natalya laughed and led them to the door. "Come back anytime." She let them pass and offered a sultry look equal to a blown kiss. "Both of you."

They said goodnight and walked back to the lift in steady silence. Once they were inside, though, Kirill swooned against the wall of the lift.

"I think I'm in love!"

Seven dropped his gaze to his shoes. "That didn't take long."

Kirill kept on shoveling praise. "She was everything you'd said she would be: clever, sophisticated. And beautiful! Oh," he said, sliding down the wall. "I want to see her again." He stood straight and grasped Seven's sleeve. "When can we see her again?"

Seven shrugged his arm free. "We just left. And this morning, you didn't even know she existed!"

"I know, but... She is so talented!" he said, letting out a groan as he fell to the wall once more.

The doors opened, and Seven took hold of Kirill's collar, hauling him up like a slack-limbed pup. "You are silly."

Kirill jerked himself free. "I'm serious! I have never felt so alive as I do tonight." He raised his head and strode out of the building and onto the street like a gallant knight of yore, grinning into the dark with his chest pushed forward as he declared, "I am a man, now." He stopped on the sidewalk and spread his arms wide. He took a deep breath for a shout, letting it out with the full power of his lungs: "Do you hear me, world? I am a man!"

Such melodrama amused, but the last thing they needed was some bothered neighbor tossing a bottle at them or calling the cops.

"Shush," Seven told him, and gave him a push to keep moving.

Kirill stepped to the car. He lowered his voice but didn't relent. "It is all thanks to you. Well, thanks to Natalya, really," he corrected himself. "But I never would have met her if it weren't for you."

"You're welcome. Now, let's go." Seven opened the driver's door and started to get in, when Kirill slapped his hand on the roof.

"I know! We'll get you a woman, too."

Seven shook his head. "That is not necessary."

"But you've done so much for me," Kirill said, almost whining. "I want to do something for you."

Seven shot him a tickled smile. "You can get in the car and let me drive."

Kirill grinned. "I can do that."

With Seven's speeding, they made it back to the hotel less than twenty minutes after curfew. Unfortunately, they couldn't sneak past Two waiting in the corridor outside the suite.

"Where have you been?" Two demanded, furrowing his bald brow. Kirill stood a head taller than him, and Seven half again as much, but Two had rank, and he wielded it like a gun. He pointed a thick finger at Kirill. "He's not supposed to be outside."

"*He* can hear you," Kirill snapped, and Seven put out his hand.

"Let me handle this." He hunched his shoulders, in deference to the senior agent. "We went into the city to blow off some steam and lost track of time. That is all." He started to move around the other man, but Two puffed his chest to block their way.

"That is not all. Your duty is to protect your charge. That includes making sure he is where he is supposed to be, at all times." Two swung his sausage finger toward Kirill again. "That boy belongs to the state—"

"I don't belong to anyone." Kirill lunged toward the stocky old agent. "And I am not a boy! I was with a *woman* tonight," he crowed suddenly. "A beautiful woman with more class and cleverness in her little finger than you have in your whole pickled little body!"

Two's dark eyes flashed at Seven. "Is this true?"

Before Seven could articulate an excuse, Kirill sneered:

"Jealous?"

"You arrogant child," Two snarled, his focus now fully on Kirill. "Go to your rooms."

"I don't take orders from you," Kirill began, when Seven stepped between them and grasped the swimmer's arms.

"Go," Seven said. "Please."

Pride and youthful belligerence shimmered in his gaze, but Kirill went, looking back just once for a sharp glare at Two. Once he was into the suite, Seven turned to Two.

"I can explain—"

"I am sure Number One will be very interested in hearing your explanations." Two pushed out his chin. "You can deliver them to his face at headquarters, first thing tomorrow morning."

The order hit Seven like a slap. "That is a four-hour drive!"

"Then I suggest you set an early alarm."

"What about Kirill?" Seven waved his arm toward the suite. "I cannot simply leave him."

"Number Nine is available. I'm sure she'll be happy to come up."

Seven balked a moment, then shook his head. "Nine is not a bodyguard."

"She's also not a self-righteous maverick with delusions of infallibility." Two edged closer, his thin lips curling back from his teeth. "You may be a decorated war hero," he said in a tone designed to intimidate, "but that carries no weight with me."

"I have never used my war record as leverage for anything," Seven said, giving a snarl. "I do not have to."

Two narrowed his stare. "See to your duty," he said at last, turning away.

Seven curled his fingers into a not-quite fist. But picking a fight with the division commander's eyes and ears in the field wasn't smart, so he let his anger go with a sigh and walked to the suite. The door was ajar, and as Seven walked in, Kirill stepped back from a hovering position.

A guilty frown replaced the athlete's former enthusiastic beam. "I'm sorry."

"Get some rest," Seven advised, in no mood for arguing or platitudes. "We both have long days tomorrow."

Chapter 3

H E LEFT KIRILL early, before the sun was up. Out in the hall, Number Nine, severe in her seriousness, stood staring at the opposite wall. Even without the telltale *IX* pin attached to her lapel, Seven would have recognized her. She'd been made famous in the ranks from the last conflict, when she'd waited belly-down in the sand for eleven days straight, subsisting only on calorie chews and water until the leader of a radical insurgents' group had stepped into just the right place for her crosshairs. That patience and single-mindedness served her well on the battlefield, but here....

"Good morning," he said, offering her a nod.

"Good morning," Nine replied, without breaking her thousand-mile stare.

Seven jerked his thumb toward the suite. "There is coffee inside."

Nine didn't move.

"They bring breakfast at 5:30," Seven said, trying once again to be cordial. "Kirill always has the same thing, but I can make sure they add something you like."

Nine's focus barely flickered. "I don't eat with my targets."

Seven approached her, head bent for a murmur. "This is not the war. He is not a target. You eat with him, talk with him, be his friend...."

She turned to him, one nostril curling up in disdain. "I suppose you let him sit in front with you when you transport him, as well?"

He drew back from that judgmental look. "Fine," he said, waving his hand. "Do it your way. I cannot be late."

Nine returned her gaze to the wall. "I'll wake him at 5."

Seven shook his head and left.

He drove to Special Security headquarters with his foot to the floor. Over four hours spent in pensive silence, followed by another hour-and-a-half in the dreary reception area while the gears of government administration ground on in painful slowness. At last, the division commander's secretary, a heavy-set woman with the beady eyes of a polecat and the hair to match, announced that Number One was ready to see him.

Seven walked into the office, a modest-sized room done in drab gray but set off by medals placed along the walls at eye-level to remind people who they were talking to. That was a smallish, hatchet-faced man at the center-placed desk, who did not rise when Seven entered. Instead, he sat reviewing some papers from over the jut of his nose for the better part of a minute before even looking up. When he did, it was only to say:

"Number Seven."

"Commander." Seven wondered if One would make him stand there at attention for this entire meeting when the old man waved a crooked hand at the chair opposite his desk.

"Sit."

Seven took the seat and kept his mouth shut. After a few moments of prolonged silence, One folded his hands in front of him and asked:

"Is there anything you'd like to say?"

"No."

One's expression betrayed no frustration or impatience, but he did prompt, "Nothing about taking your charge off secure grounds and failing to return him to his rooms before curfew?"

Seven shrugged. "You seem to know the details already. Why should I repeat them?"

The old man twitched. Just a tic at the corner of his mouth, but the façade had been broken. "No one is ever as clever as he thinks he is."

"I never claimed to be clever," Seven said.

"Your job is to protect Morozov."

"I was with him the whole time."

"Number Two said you took him to a whore. Did you hold his hand while he screwed her?"

Seven's spine reacted with an itch. Not so much for the words, but for their inflection. "Number Two was not there."

One raised his chin in an effort to look down his nose. It half-worked. "So, tell me what happened."

Seven drew a breath and released it again. "We went into the city; that is true. And, we met a woman. That is also true."

"A prostitute," One said.

Seven tilted his head.

"You can tell me now," One said, jowls drooping. "Or, I can dispatch an investigator."

"An escort," Seven relented. "But, she is very tactful. I trust her."

"That's not the point. Morozov cannot be wasting his DNA on some overpriced whore."

Seven pulled a face. "He 'wastes his DNA' every time he steps under the shower!"

One drew his thin lips taut, and Seven backpedaled.

"He is twenty-two years old. It was just a bit of fun. He has been kept under lock and key since he was a boy—"

"For good reason! Do you know how many years – how much *money* – we have spent cultivating young men and women like him? These are not mere athletes," One said gravely. "They are warriors: the strongest, fastest, fiercest warriors who will restore our country to its great glory. Which we never would have lost if we had stayed pure. They may have barred us from the last Games, but that will not happen again. Morozov will win." He pointed a finger at Seven. "You will make certain it happens."

"I cannot simply deny him his freedom," Seven said, when One cut him off again.

"You can, and you will."

Seven stared at him, struck momentarily silent by the director's authoritarian fervor. "And if he says no?"

One scoffed. "A dog that cannot be brought to heel must be punished." His bushy brows went up. "Is that what you want? To have him punished for a bit of fun?"

Seven shifted his jaw to the left, then the right, then mumbled, "No."

"No," One echoed in contempt. His gaze remained firm as he leaned against his chair with an air of satisfaction. "Now that we understand each other, I expect a full report on events to date before you return to your assignment." He looked down at his desk, grasped a file folder, and opened it up for perusal. "See my secretary; she will supply you with the necessary forms and a typewriter." He glanced up again, but only for a moment, and only to say, "Dismissed."

Seven forced himself up and went for the door. He pushed it open without shoving, though only just barely, and walked briskly past the polecat. Before she made him stop for those stupid forms, he held up his hand and snapped, "I need the head." She grunted at his back but articulated nothing, and he continued down the corridor. By the time he got to the lavatory, his steps were stomping. The lav door he did shove; it banged against the wall, creating a crack of splintering tile.

At the sink, he splashed himself with cold water, and in the mirror, his good eye took in his reflection. The water ran down his face, following and catching in the lines of the scar marring the left side, including the eye that had gone gray and dead from an unlucky shrapnel shard. The war had taken a lot from him. Less than some and more than others, but he'd been able to hold his wounded head high knowing that what he'd lost, he'd lost for the sake of his country's people. That included Kirill.

Seven drew a few centering breaths, relieved himself, and returned to the polecat. His brusqueness from earlier didn't go over well because she told him to sit and then made him wait for forty-five minutes before she led him down two hallways, a staircase, and another hallway to a tiny cubicle lit with a flickering fluorescent overhead. A single desk with a typewriter took up most of the space; there was barely enough room for Seven to pull out the lone chair to sit down.

His only course of action was to do One's busy work. It took a few hours, and when he'd finished, the polecat was out at her lunch. Seven decided to walk outside for some food, himself, but everywhere he went, it was too busy, too expensive, or too unappetizing. In the end, he waited in a half-hour-long queue at a café for a bowl of soup that wasn't half-bad but also wasn't very good, either. Then it was back to the main office, where the polecat made him wait yet again. This time, he decided to loom in a towering at-ease position in front of her desk. She still took nearly fifteen minutes before she acknowledged him.

"All right," she said, and put out her hand.

Seven passed her the report. She gave it a single glance, and said:

"You need to redo it."

"You are joking," Seven hoped.

She pushed the papers back to him. "You can't type over the lines. It distorts the scanner."

"That is bullshit," Seven blurted before he could stop himself.

The polecat scowled. "Do you want the new forms or not? It makes no difference to me."

Seven bit back the barb at the tip of his tongue and held out his hand, snatching the blank forms between his fingers.

It took another hour to type the new report, and another hour after that to get it approved. By the time he'd finished at headquarters, he was famished, but the cafe he'd gone to at lunch was mobbed with tourists, and it was already evening. He settled for a travel coffee and a pork sandwich so tasteless and terrible that he tossed it out the car window after three bites for some stray to find later.

It was past lights-out when he finally got back to the hotel complex. He'd lurched his way nearly to the lifts when he heard Number Two say from somewhere off his blind side:

"How was headquarters?"

Seven barely managed to hold in his contempt as he turned to the other agent. "Do you miss it? You can go back, you know. We can handle things here without you."

Two dropped his forced congeniality. "The only reason you still have this assignment is because the Games are so close. Once Morozov wins his golds, your days are numbered."

"Just like the rest of me," Seven said, waggling his lapel with its *VII* pin.

Two drew a breath to wrinkle his nose, which he lifted at Seven in an authoritarian sniff. "See to your charge. I don't want to have to talk to you again." He walked off with his hands clasped behind him like a despotic headmaster.

"You think I want that either?" Seven muttered at his back, late and low enough not to be heard. His limbs felt like lead, but he didn't go up to the suite. First, he needed a drink.

He walked into the hotel bar, pulled up to a seat in front of the bartender, and ordered a shot of whisky, which he knocked back all at once when the bartender set it in front of him. It went down harshly, not like the good stuff Natalya had.

He pulled out his phone and scrolled to a familiar number.

Dear Cleopatra, he typed. *Will you see Antony?*

He set the phone down on the bar. In less time than it took for him to order a second whisky, the phone buzzed with a reply.

A queen's nights have too many hours to say no.

Seven smiled to himself and tossed back the second whisky. Because to hell with men like Number One and his cronies, who thought they could control other people's lives.

Chapter 4

WAKING EARLY WAS a helpful habit for guarding an athlete who started a rigid training schedule before six in the morning, though the previous day's frustrations left Seven bleary-eyed when his alarm went off. Regardless, he got out of bed, did his push-ups, and jumped into a fast shower, to be alert and ready before the breakfast trays arrived.

He was expecting Kirill to stumble up from bed just in time to eat. But today, the swimmer was already in the main room waiting for him while Seven was still fin-ger-drying his brush cut.

"You're back!" Kirill greeted with a gleaming grin. "I'm so glad you're back."

Seven chuckled. "I was only gone for a day."

"It felt like a week! That Nine has no imagination." Kirill pulled a sour face and mimed the flipping of a switch. "9:30. Lights out."

The impression, however unfavorable, was too accu-rate, and Seven laughed. Kirill did, too, briefly. Then he turned serious.

"I'm sorry I got you in trouble—"

Seven waved him off. "It's all right."

"No." Kirill stepped forward. "You have always been kind to me, when to everyone else I have been a...a commodity. You've always been my friend." He bowed his head. "I shot my mouth off in front of that vindictive little lizard, and you paid the price."

"It's fine," Seven repeated, laying his hand on Kirill's shoulder for a pat. "Really." The swimmer looked up, guardedly hopeful, and Seven offered him a tight smile. "It's my job to look after you. That includes keeping you safe from vindictive little lizards." He gave Kirill's shoulder a solid, prodding shake, and smiled wider. "And returning you to your queen."

Perhaps it was only a trick of the light as his gaze popped wide, but the gold in Kirill's eyes flashed suddenly bright. "Natalya?" he asked, in a voice hushed for excitement, and Seven nodded. "When?"

"Tonight, if you are willing."

A wave of warm emotion flowed over Kirill's young face before being replaced by a look of concern. "But, Number Two...! How will I—?"

"Until you are in chains, you are no prisoner." Seven tweaked his smile. "I will take care of you."

Kirill smiled back. "You always do," he said as breakfast arrived. As soon as the porter left, he poured a cup of coffee and handed it to Seven.

"Thank you," Kirill said, leaving Seven slightly dumb for a moment. "If there is ever anything I can do to repay you...?"

Seven took the coffee with another chuckle. "It's just a date," he said, choosing not to articulate his more sentimental answer, that Kirill's happiness was payment enough for any risk he might take.

That evening, Natalya was almost as magnanimous when she met them at her door.

"My prince!" she said, opening her arms. They were bare, save for a cluster of delicate gold bracelets wrapped around her left wrist. Her legs were bare, too; her tan, wraparound dress was little more than a toga covering her essentials. It covered with voluptuous elegance, though, enough to make Kirill stare.

His interest didn't go unmarked.

"You like the dress?" she guessed.

"It's very beautiful," Kirill said, finding his voice. "Though, not as beautiful as you."

Natalya crooned a low, "Oh," and caressed his cheek. "You are sweet." She moved her hand to his shoulder and drew him inside. "Come! I have much to teach you tonight."

Seven's gut tightened at her words, but as he followed them in and closed the door behind him, he was met with a different scene than he was expecting.

The apartment was lit with surprising brightness, and soft music played from speakers tucked into the corners of the main room. He recognized the famous sweeping measures of the waltz from Tchaikovsky's Sleeping Beauty. Natalya's hips and shoulders flowed in time to the music as she walked over to the wet bar by the windows. She picked up two tumblers of reddish whisky and gave one to Kirill and the other to Seven, humming as she did so. When Kirill bent his head to sniff at the drink, Natalya raised her hand.

"Not yet!"

Around the room, the waltz came to a stop. Natalya did as well, with her chin high and her arms at her sides, with the poise of a prima ballerina.

"Last time," she said to Kirill in a tone of officious instruction befitting a master choreographer, "was your orientation. Tonight, your education begins in earnest." She turned away to the bar, where she swept up a third waiting tumbler of whisky, at the same time continuing with her lecture.

"Of course," she said, "there are women you can just toss onto a bed and have your way with. But those are vapid playthings, with no minds of their own. Real women, the ones worth having, must be won by degrees."

She returned to them and raised her glass almost to her lips, keeping her gaze on Kirill. "Drink slowly," she directed, "but without hesitation. And, look into her eyes when you do. Imagine it is her on your lips: her smoothness, her heat, her complexity. She will feel that intensity from across a room."

Ever responsive to her orders, Kirill tipped the glass to his lips. He kept his eyes trained on Natalya, the gold flecks there shimmering like the whisky in his glass, or like stars on a cloudless night. His forceful swallow belied some surprise at the burn, but Seven didn't snicker. Instead, he watched with great interest as a mature sensuality bloomed in the younger man's face. It pulled at him, and for a moment Seven forgot where they were and why they were here, until Natalya let out a delighted laugh.

"Bravo!" She shimmied her shoulders, her nipples straining suddenly erect against her dress. "I felt that in my toes!"

A blush filled Kirill's cheeks, and he glanced at his feet. Seven did, too, sipping the warm whisky to soothe his dry tongue.

Natalya came between them, reaching for Kirill's glass. "We're not finished, yet." She set the glass on the table and picked up a tiny remote control, and Tchaikovsky started up again. She turned to Kirill and extended her arm, as though in welcome. "Now, we waltz."

Kirill burst with a sudden laugh. "I don't know how to waltz!"

"Of course, you do," Natalya said matter-of-factly. "The waltz is in our blood. Even this one knows." She tipped her head at Seven, who agreed from behind his glass.

"Prove it," Kirill challenged with a smile.

Seven took another sip of his whisky before setting it beside Kirill's on the table, then stood at attention. At his beckoning, Natalya stepped into his space and put her arms around him.

He led them in a box step, counting out the movements – *step, side, close; step, side, close* – in three-quarter-time. It felt strange to be dancing with her again, like he was in a dream. The last time, he'd been a new soldier, in his new uniform, blushing beneath the lights of the dance hall. He'd always been big, his size off-putting to smaller boys and a threat to their bullies. But Natalya had clicked up to him at that ball in her delicate heels and poofy dress and told him she was proud of him. Then as now, he looked not at their feet but at her face, the way trusting dancers were supposed to do, and smiled at the green gleam of her eyes, feeling weightless and free.

"I never knew you were so graceful!"

Kirill's tickled outburst yanked Seven back to the present. He stopped and stepped out of Natalya's arms, facing the swimmer with a frown.

"You think you are so much better, let us see you try."

Cued by the goad, Natalya walked to Kirill and took his hands, to lead them into proper place.

"A dance is the fastest way to put a woman in your arms," she said as she moved into starting position with him. She pressed her lips into a new, knowing smile. "And if she wants to stay in your arms, she will want to stay in your bed."

That sobered Kirill, who drew a breath that straightened and tightened his posture. He followed Natalya's instructions as she forced him to take the lead. His athletic agility and muscle control made him a swift learner, and very quickly his feet became more confident. His hands, too, as they moved around her with greater intimacy. Natalya encouraged him, closing her embrace around him until their bodies touched.

Seven cleared his throat.

Kirill jerked his head up and stepped back from Natalya. A fresh burn rushed into his face and he glanced down at his groin. Seven didn't need to follow his focus. Neither did Natalya, who chuckled and said:

"Such is the magic of the dance! Don't worry; we'll take care of that." She waved Kirill toward the bedroom. "Go on. I'll be with you in a moment."

Kirill went into the bedroom, trying to hide his arousal with an awkward hunch. As the door clicked closed, Seven shook his head.

"I was not aware," he said to Natalya in a side-of-his-mouth mutter, "that your business included drinking and dancing lessons."

She clicked her tongue and swayed close to keep their volume low. "How a man drinks a whisky will show you how patient he is. And how he dances a waltz, how kind."

"And, how do I compare?"

"You do both very well," she said, with just a hint of false flattery. "Though I could still teach you a few things."

"No doubt." He reached into the inside pocket of his jacket, but she stopped his hand before he could complete the motion.

"Keep your money," she said, her voice going quiet again.

He stared at her, somewhat uneasily. "I cannot owe you that many favors."

Natalya's expression held no guile. "You owe me nothing. I consider it a privilege to help shape a young, strong man. Usually, they come to me lonely and sad, the victims of their own ambition, when the only woman who will listen is one they have to pay." She smiled again, this time in mischief. "Besides, our young prince's attention does wonders for my ego."

He laughed, but it quickly died as the corners of her mouth lost some of their wicked mirth and she whispered:

"And, I like being part of your life again."

He searched her eyes for the tease. There was none, so he bowed his head to admit, "I like it, too."

She held his gaze for a long moment, then broke into a chuckle that released them both from any deeper sentimentality.

"I should not keep my student waiting," she said.

"No," Seven agreed wryly. "He might explode."

She patted him on the cheek. "Be a good guard dog and have a nap on the sofa?"

Seven pulled his mouth to one side. "Woof."

Natalya laughed in her winsome way and turned with a swing of her hips, leaving him to savor the whisky and waltz while she furthered Kirill's education.

Such lessons continued over the next several weeks. While they always included sex, they weren't always about it; Natalya seemed to take genuine delight in teaching Kirill about refinement, etiquette, and poise. Once, she even had a tailor waiting for them, to fit Kirill with a stylish ensemble that made him look like the modern-day prince she called him.

Seven was careful to coordinate these sessions with group outings into the city, to stay under Number Two's radar. He and Kirill would quickly veer from the rest of the group, sometimes as soon as they drove into the tunnel to the city, but so long as they were back before curfew, no one was any the wiser. No one took any extra notice of them, in fact. Or so Seven thought.

As he stood outside the locker room one evening, waiting for Kirill to finish getting ready for another meet with Natalya, Seven became alert to the clack of heels on the tile and the faint waft of women's perfume. Usually, the other athletes paid him as much attention as they would a piece of furniture or a switch on the wall. This time, though, one of them walked straight up to him, stopped by his side, and offered him a smile. It was Darya Vikhrova, she of the perfect dive, dressed to kill in a tight black outfit that accentuated her athletic curves, which even he had to admit were very impressive.

"Hello," she said, leaving the syllables in the air as a prompt.

"Hello." He tried his best to keep from glancing at her cleavage, but it was very distracting. "Can I help you?"

"Where is Kirill?" she asked, shifting her posture to peer around his arm.

"Fixing his hair."

She kept up her curious scrutiny of the door and locker room beyond, musing, "He's different, lately." She flicked her focus up to him. Her eyes were a mix of blue and gray, he noticed, the dominant color changing depending on how they caught the light. At the moment, the blue commanded, sparkling like the sea. "And, he always disappears when he comes out with us. Why is that?"

"He is Batman," Seven told her drily.

Her lips weren't painted, but their gloss shimmered as she pulled them into a tiny smile. "He's not that mysterious. Not like you." She passed her gaze over him – all over him – before settling back on his face. "How old are you?"

"Thirty-six."

She popped her slender brows. "You don't look that old."

He snorted in amusement. "Thank you."

She squinted. "You weren't with Kirill for the last Games."

"No. I was assigned just after."

Darya made a strange noise filled with regret, awe, and exasperation. "He would have won that year, I think." Her expression became fully irritated as she added, "If the committee had let any of us compete. He'll win this year, though." Her eyes gleamed. "I will, too. And as soon as they give me my gold, I'm going to jump off that medalist's platform straight onto a plane for Italy."

"Italy?" he echoed with interest.

She nodded. "There is a little town on the coast where tourists sunbathe and spend their money to watch divers leap from the great cliff into the warm blue ocean." Her voice took on an impassioned growl. "I'm going to teach all the little girls who have been told their whole lives that they are nothing that if they can do a perfect dive from that cliff, they can have *every-thing*."

Her passion infected, and he smiled. "That sounds like a nice dream."

"It would be nicer," Darya said, her voice becoming a purr, "with a big, strong man like you around." She drifted close enough to walk her fingers along his lapel. "During the day, you could watch me dive. And at night, we could drink wine, and eat gelato, and swim naked with the dolphins in the sea."

He snickered. "You forgot making love on a moonlit beach."

Her eyes shimmered. "We could do that, too. In fact," she said with breathy intent, "we don't even need the beach. You have a private suite right upstairs."

"That is Kirill's."

"He can come, too." She pushed herself closer, her firm breasts pressing against his ribs. "What do you say?"

Seven took hold of her hand, halting its progress to his shoulder, and eased away. "I don't think so."

She stepped back, too, blinking rapidly. A short, sharp, incredulous laugh escaped her. "I don't understand?"

"No," Seven agreed, shaking his head. "You wouldn't."

Darya straightened up, chin high and defiant. Her eyes flashed, the cold gray taking hold. "You think me a child?"

"No," he said again. "I think you are a bold, determined young woman. I am simply not fascinated. Now, please, go back to your teammates before Fourteen notices you are gone."

Her lower lip quivered a moment, then she snapped her mouth shut and whirled about, the fan of her ponytail and the angry staccato of her shoes her only riposte.

Seven sighed after her and turned to the locker room opening, only to find Kirill standing there staring at him. "What?" he prompted.

Kirill lunged toward him, his expression suddenly desperate. "Are you crazy?"

"What?" Seven repeated, furrowing his brows.

"She just invited *both* of us upstairs!" Kirill wheezed. "And you sent her away!"

Seven wrinkled his nose. "She was looking for attention, not a gang bang."

"How do you know?"

"Because I listened to her," Seven said, still snapping. "She is angry, and lonely, and to take advantage of that is not a trait of a gentleman. Besides," he sneered, "I thought you were already in love with Natalya."

Kirill shrank back, shifting his mouth from one side to the other. He dropped his gaze to his shoes – expensive, calfskin leather oxfords gifted to him from Natalya herself less than a week ago – and fell silent for a long, uneasy minute.

That wretched, downtrodden look made Seven blow out his frustration in another sigh. "Do you still want to see Natalya?" he asked in a calmer murmur, because that precious young man's ego would need some new stroking.

"Yes," Kirill mumbled.

Seven tilted his head down the corridor. "Come on, then," he said, and started walking without waiting. Kirill caught up to him within five long strides.

They were in the car before either spoke, and even that was just another mumble from Kirill.

"I'm sorry."

Seven waved his fingers up from the steering wheel. "Forget it."

Another long silence followed, this one pregnant with uncertainty. They were speeding over the bridge to the city before Kirill broke it again, his voice still tentative.

"What did she say?"

"Just that she wants to get out," Seven said. He kept his eyes on the road but rubbed one hand over his brow; ever since his trip to headquarters, he'd had similar feelings. There was the young man in the seat beside him to think about, though, which Seven did, all the time.

Kirill's clothes squeaked against his seat as he slouched into it. "She hates this life, doesn't she?"

Seven left the question unanswered, focusing on the turns and traffic as they merged onto the southbound highway.

"Do you think she hates me, too?" Kirill asked.

Seven relented with a shake of his head. "No." He couldn't keep himself from cracking a quick smile. "She thinks you are Batman."

"Really?" Kirill's voice swung up, and he rose forward in his seat. "Batman is cool."

"He is also make-believe. You are a real man." Seven looked at him, at his fine, young face full of pride and promise, and felt a rush of emotion. "A good one."

Kirill smiled. "So are you," he said.

Seven turned back to the road, hoping Kirill wouldn't see his blush, when the air popped in his ears and a bolt of fire exploded less than a dozen cars in front of them.

Chapter 5

ONE VEHICLE FLEW into the air; another flipped over its side like a twisting diver launching from a board. Seven wrenched their car away from the ballooning fire, narrowly missing a sidelong-screeching truck in the outer lane when a compact slammed into their rear bumper, sending their sedan spinning.

They smashed into a line of already-crashed, crunched vehicles. Seven heard his head crack against the steering wheel. He jolted up again and looked at Kirill, who was rising slowly from a bracing position with his hands thrust out to the dash. His hair stuck out at shocked angles and his skin gleamed clammy-white, but otherwise he seemed all right.

Seven still had to check. "Are you hurt?"

"I don't think so...?" Kirill's pupils loomed large in his eyes, and it took him a moment to focus. "You're bleeding."

Seven touched his forehead; his fingers came back with a smear of blood. He felt his dead eye squinting and blinking, and he wiped what he hoped was a clearer path across his skin.

Shouts and screaming filtered through the cracks in the chassis and the waning tinnitus in his ears. He could feel a wafting heat, too, from the exploded car and one that had begun to burn beside it.

He slapped the catch of his safety belt. "We have to go."

Kirill sat dazed, and Seven shouted his name. The swimmer blinked in rapid succession but didn't move.

Seven reached over and wrestled with the passenger safety belt lock, his fingers fumbling against the awkward angle.

"We have to get out of here," he repeated as the latch came free and retracted across Kirill's chest. "Does your door work?"

Kirill had started to come around. He jerked at the handle, but the door didn't budge. A shove with his shoulder yielded the same lacking result. "No...!"

Seven tried his own door. It creaked with give. He twisted around in the car, got his leg out from under the dash, and kicked the door hard with his heel. It squealed and swung outward on protesting hinges.

"This way," he said, shimmying out legs-first.

Kirill's agility proved itself well as he clambered over the gearshift and driver's seat. As soon as he was out, Seven hauled him nearly under his arm, throwing his gaze in all directions to assess the situation.

"Code Red," he barked for sake of his comm, following with their location.

The voice of Control came back in his ear, clipped but restrained. "Are you compromised?"

Seven grimaced at their vehicle. "Our car is."

"Emergency crews have been alerted," Control told him. "Secure your assignment and await instructions."

The comm clicked off in his ear, and Seven swore to himself. On their own, then. He didn't dare pull his gun in this chaos, but he touched its butt to make sure it was still safe under his arm.

He pushed Kirill ahead of him and pointed up the block. "Go."

"To where?"

"Natalya's. It's secure, and I trust her." He hurried three steps, but Kirill didn't keep pace. "What are you waiting for? Come on!"

Kirill waved an arm toward the pile of wrecked traffic. "What about those people? And Darya? She was coming this way, too, with the others. We have to make sure they're okay!"

Seven hustled back and grabbed his arm. "If we come across any of them before we get to Natalya's, we'll take them with us. But you are my first priority," he said, and gave Kirill the mightiest shove yet. The younger man came along at half-again pace, this time without protest. That was good, because the blood dripping from Seven's head was getting worse – he tasted its sharp, salty flow on his lips – and the streets had started to turn mad.

They found an alley between a grocer and a coffee shop, where Seven cleaned his face. His hands stayed smeared, though, even after he wiped them on his trousers.

"Here," Kirill muttered, pulling off his tie. It was a pretty silk make, and Seven hated to mess it. At least it was a dark color.

He wadded the tie into a compact ball that he pressed to his head, once and again. He flashed a more conscious look into the street to get his bearings. Natalya's apartment complex was dozens of blocks away...but these were city blocks, short and straight and easy to navigate. He'd done it plenty of times in his youth.

"Can you run?" he asked Kirill.

The swimmer nodded confidently. "What about you?"

Seven tucked the tie into his jacket pocket. "I will be right behind you."

"Promise?"

"Yes. Now, go!" Seven said, pushing him into the street with the gut-clenching feeling that he was back on a battlefield.

They got to the high rise without trouble and without seeing anyone else they knew. Seven was glad they didn't have to stop. Alarms had been raised, and even at this distance away, he could hear the faint wail of emergency sirens echoing between the city blocks.

He jabbed the intercom button for her apartment. There was a telltale hiss of air indicating an open connection, followed by a gasp. Natalya's cultured façade was broken by a sailor's curse that actually made Seven break into a smile.

"What happened?" she demanded.

"I'll explain after you let us up," he said, and the door buzzed in quick reply. He maneuvered Kirill inside and went in behind him, closing the outer door firmly after them.

Natalya was waiting at her apartment door, in a draping dress with a deep arcing cut in the top and a high arcing cut in the bottom, a glamorous sight that clashed with the fear on her face. She crossed to Seven, wheezing, "Semyon!" Her slender fingers grazed his temple, and he cringed.

"It's fine."

She stood straight with a humph. "What in God's name have you gotten yourself into, this time?"

"There was an explosion," Kirill said, "on the side of the road. It took out our car. This was the safest place we could come...!"

"All right, all right." Natalya drew them inside and tsked at Seven. "Let's clean you up."

The apartment was warm and quiet and dim. Seven made his way to the sofa, where Kirill helped him sit. Natalya swept down next to him, a little red bag in one hand and a bottle in the other. Unfortunately, the bottle was peroxide, not whisky, and Seven hissed when she pressed a cotton ball full of the stuff to his face.

"I thought you said it was fine," she said.

"It still burns!" He could also hear it fizzing.

"You're being a baby," Natalya scolded as she made several more liberal dabs.

Standing to the side, Kirill rubbed his hands. "Can I do something?"

"You can get me a drink," Seven said. "Whisky."

Kirill went to the bar, and Natalya continued to clean the wound. Seven leaned back against the cushions with a tight-lipped groan. He tried to relax, leaving his gaze to wander. It was drawn to Natalya's chest, the most defined thing in his vision, and the delicate silver-and-diamond necklace nestled there.

"That is very pretty," he muttered. "Your necklace."

She hummed. "It was a gift from a foreign ambassador who has a fondness for fine ballet." As she reached for a bandage, he caught her quick smirk. "And wicked women to watch it with."

Seven chuckled, and over her shoulder he caught sight of Kirill. Hovering at the side of the sofa, he looked very disheveled, very worried, and very sweet.

"Does it hurt?" he asked.

Seven nodded for the glass. "It won't after that." He took a cautious sip and sucked some air between his teeth as chaser. "Now, *that* is a good burn."

Natalya finished and got up with the bag, and Kirill took her place. He peered at Seven's face. "It doesn't look so bad."

"One more scar won't matter." Seven snickered. "I am already ugly."

"No, you're not," Kirill said, in a hushed and gentle voice.

Seven's easy humor fell away as he met the younger man's gaze, where an unexpected seriousness that was almost melancholy flickered. He didn't have time to analyze or question it, though, for a breezy interruption from Natalya.

"You boys are darling," she said, sitting down on the arm of the sofa next to Seven. "But have you figured out, yet, how you're going to get home without a car?"

Seven frowned. "I will think of something."

She swept up again with a swirl of satin and a har-rumph. "While you think, I will do."

"Natalya," he began, but she had already plucked her phone from the table and was navigating the menus deftly with her thumb.

"My ambassador friend will be happy to help." She put the phone to her ear with a naughty smile. "He enjoys me being indebted to him."

"Natalya!" Seven protested again.

She shushed him. "Don't argue. You know better than that."

As Natalya put on a wide smile to be heard in her voice, Kirill watched her in mystified amazement. "Can she really do that?" he asked. "Get us a car from a foreign embassy?"

Seven sighed. "I have never known her to not be able to do what she says she will do," he said, while Natalya laughed, cajoled, and made her deals over the phone.

Kirill's voice wafted close to his ear, softer than the cotton Natalya had pressed to his skin just a few minutes ago. "Do you love her?"

Seven looked into that fine face so smooth with youth and caught his breath. But, once again, Natalya insinuated herself into the moment with a dramatic swoop of skirt. She came down beside Seven and patted him on the leg.

"Your car is on the way," she said.

Seven replied in the only appropriate fashion. "Thank you."

"You're welcome." She shrugged. "Of course, it means you cannot stay."

He hummed. "It was not the evening any of us was expecting."

"No." She extended a hand across Seven's chest to Kirill. "My brave prince," she said, gripping his fingers. "I'm sorry to have disappointed you."

Kirill held her hand, but loosely. "You could never be a disappointment," he said, and Natalya cooed, while Seven tried to make himself smaller between them.

She noticed his fidgeting and narrowed her eyes for another shrewd smile. "You will take care of this big one, yes? Until we meet again?"

"I would be proud to do so half as well as you," Kirill said, which caused Natalya to stretch her shoulders in flattered delight.

"You sweet thing!" She rose and drew him to standing, too, so she could move up against him with the promise of feminine fulfilment. "Be safe; be strong; and come back to me sometime." And, putting her arms around him, she kissed him with the practiced sensuality of her occupation.

When they parted, Seven stood with them. "I'm sorry," he began, when Natalya clucked another scold at him.

"Don't you dare! I'm proud you came to me." She stroked the scarred side of his face, tingling the nerves under his skin. "And, I enjoyed being your Florence Nightingale, this time," she said, kissing him on his good cheek.

She saw them to the lift. Once the doors had closed, Seven told Control that they'd secured transport and were headed back to the training complex. The voice on the other end confirmed, and when Seven asked about the others, Control informed him that Number Fourteen and her athletes were on their way back, and Number Twelve already had the rest of the men's team in lockdown in their rooms, which was precisely where Seven and Kirill were expected to go, too, as soon as they arrived.

In the lobby, a thin, dark man in a solid black suit greeted them. "Are you Natalya's friends?" he asked, and Seven nodded. The driver introduced himself as Alex and extended his arm toward the doors. "This way, please."

Alex took them to a dark blue, roomy sedan parked out front with the hazards blinking. He opened the rear door, and Seven urged Kirill inside before following. Alex took the driver's seat and, once they were on the road, asked them to confirm the address for his GPS. Seven did so, and the driver made a noise of clarification.

"We'll have to take a detour from the main roads. There was an explosion earlier."

"We heard," Seven said, avoiding any more detail. "Was anyone hurt?"

"Nothing reported. But it's caused a right mess of traffic." Alex smiled over his shoulder. "Feel free to relax back there."

Seven thanked him and sat back against the leather interior. The back seat was a novelty for him, and he took the time to enjoy the feeling of distraction that belonged to a passenger. He was about to comment on this to Kirill, when he noticed the younger man staring morosely out his window.

Seven leaned toward him, whispering, "Control says the others are safe. And we will be with them soon."

"Okay," Kirill said, and turned back to his window.

Seven decided not to press. Kirill was silent for the rest of the drive.

When they arrived at the hotel, Alex opened the car door for them, looked up at the complex, and whistled.

"Impressive! I didn't know this was even out here."

"It is for the athletes," Seven said. "Kirill is a swimmer, training for the Games."

"Really?" Alex smiled. "Can I say I met you, if you win?"

Kirill didn't react beyond a blink, so Seven said, "There is little doubt of that. This one is a champion."

Alex was polite enough not to poke. "You must be very proud," he said to Seven, who agreed. "Well, good luck with your training." He put out his hand. "It was nice to meet you. Any friend of Natalya's...."

"Thank you," Seven said again, and shook. He bade Alex farewell and turned Kirill toward the hotel.

As soon as they were inside the main doors, Number Two strode up, pointing a finger at them. "You!"

Seven held up his hand before Two could say anything more. "Tomorrow."

The older agent kept yammering. "There has been a breach of security. He needs to be debriefed—"

"Tomorrow," Seven repeated with a menacing lean. "He has been through enough tonight." He pushed Kirill in front of him, directing him toward the lifts.

Two sputtered after them. "I will inform Number One about this!"

"Go ahead," Seven mumbled, as he and Kirill walked into a waiting lift. The doors closed; thankfully, Two didn't follow. In the hush, Seven muttered, "I am sorry tonight did not go as planned."

Kirill slumped against the wall. "It's not your fault."

Seven watched him a moment before trying again. "Are you all right?"

"Fine," Kirill said, though he stayed slouched, shuffling down the corridor with his hands in his pockets when they came to their floor.

Seven let them into the suite and locked the door with two sharp clicks and a swing of the deadbolt.

"The lockdown is only a precaution," he explained. "Until things settle down."

"I understand," Kirill said dully.

Seven sighed. In the safety of the suite, he could assert himself better than he could in the car or the lift. "Tell me what is wrong."

Kirill turned and looked up from between his slumping shoulders. "Do you think I am terrible?"

"No." Seven squinted at him. "Why would you think that?"

"You have taken care of me for over three years," Kirill said, his voice cracking with guilt. "Yet, I have never once asked your name."

Seven blew a sigh. "You know my name."

"Natalya called you Semyon—"

"That name is not who I am anymore," Seven told him.

"Then who was he?" Kirill planted himself on the sofa. "I want to know," he said, his eyes flashing with determination.

Seven sighed again and sat down on the opposite side of the sofa. This story was common record in the military files, but he'd never actually told it to anyone. He pulled out his earpiece and tucked it into his pocket so it was out of range of his voice.

"I was a young soldier," he began, "sent to fight a war. My squad was on recon one day, not far from the border. There were lots of abandoned vehicles, and trash everywhere. We'd gotten used to it. But we didn't know that one of the cars had been rigged with a bomb." An abrupt sense-memory of explosive heat made him blink. "Our sergeant was closest when it went off. Somehow, he was still alive." Another blink, as he recalled the man's ear-splitting howling. "Another soldier and I pulled him to cover. The rest of them were panicking, shouting and firing in all directions." He shrugged to himself. "Most of them were just boys. Then, another car exploded."

For a heartbeat, he was there again: smoke burning his eyes, fire singeing his nostrils, and the Babel-esque shouts of his comrades filling his ears. And Leon: skinny, twenty-year-old Leon, wide-eyed and white-faced in frozen shock, with the line of cars burning behind him.

Seven never remembered exactly what had come next, but he'd been told: How he'd bolted from his sergeant and screamed for Leon when another explosion eradicated almost a third of that young soldier's body. The shrapnel shard that pierced his own face hadn't stopped him from dragging Leon to safety, though, an act for which they'd called him a hero, when all Seven had really tried to do was to keep his comrade from dying out there, alone and so far from home.

He relayed the details of the story in the same matter-of-fact manner used by the army officer at his discharge meeting. No one in that room had asked the question, but Kirill did:

"Were you afraid?"

Seven smiled wryly. "I could not have survived any of that without being afraid. I think it is why I don't remember it very clearly."

"What happened then?"

"I woke up in a field hospital." Seven recalled suddenly the kind, clear, green-blue eyes watching over him in his convalescent bed. "To the most beautiful nurse, with the most soothing voice I'd ever heard, and the most caring touch I've ever felt."

Kirill smiled knowingly. "Natalya?" he said, but Seven laughed.

"No! No, Natalya's bedside manner has always been better suited to more...private situations."

Kirill's smile fractured at Seven's laughter, but the curious interest in his gaze remained intact. "So, who was your beautiful nurse, then?"

That brought a pause, and an anxious cramping in his underbelly. Even fewer knew this story. But the shine in Kirill's eyes was too bright, too attentive, too splendid to ignore.

"His name was Erik." The name sounded almost mystical to Seven's ears; he hadn't said it aloud in years. "The first night after I woke, he stayed by my side and held my hand, and listened to me cry. He let me be sad for my comrades, and angry over my eye. Then, he told me that, while I could not go back, and that it would take time, I would become strong again." Those remembered words prompted a melancholy smile. "And, I did."

He looked over at Kirill, not knowing what to expect. Surprise, perhaps, or revulsion. But the swimmer's gaze gleamed only with interest.

"What happened to him?" Kirill asked, and Seven opened his hands.

"I have no idea. When I was healed enough, they sent me home."

Kirill sat forward. "He did not go with you?"

Seven laughed again, softly. "To him, I was just another wounded trooper. I doubt, if you asked him now, he would even remember my name. But I will always remember his."

"So, you never told him how you felt?" Kirill asked, in a quiet but confident way that sounded like he already knew the answer.

"I was never that brave." Seven sat back, that sad part of the story over. "After I came home, the Security Division was recruiting. Even with my eye, I had a good record. So, I applied, and they accepted me."

"That's when you became Seven?" Kirill asked.

"Number Seven, yes."

Kirill slumped, but Seven offered him a smile.

"Don't look so sad. I could have been assigned some stuffy businessman or self-important politician. Instead, I was given a thoughtful and charming young man, who keeps me on my toes and makes me laugh."

That brought a tiny smile to Kirill's face. After a moment, he asked, "Does Natalya know? About...?"

"She is the only one who does." Seven chuckled half-heartedly. "Until now, of course."

Kirill bowed his head. "I will not tell anyone," he said, softly but with a conviction that pitched his voice suddenly deep.

Seven smiled his appreciation. The moment didn't seem to need more than that.

"She's a good friend to you?" Kirill guessed, his voice reverting to its natural lively tone.

Seven nodded. "My oldest and dearest."

"And you love her?"

"Not like you do," Seven said.

Kirill shook his head. "She does not love me," he said with serious sincerity. "Not that I thought that was a possibility. I know what she does. But, tonight, it was obvious." His gaze became clear and full of resigned awareness. "She loves you."

Seven drew a breath to contradict, but Kirill stopped him.

"It's all right. I do not blame her!" The younger man shrugged, without anger or sorrow. "Sometimes, we cannot help who we love, yes?" He paused and glanced away for a thought. "But," he resumed after a moment, "I want to be with a woman who feels the same way about me that I feel about her."

The ingenuousness in those eyes made Seven swallow and nod. "That is very mature."

Kirill smiled and dropped his gaze for a sudden blooming blush. It flashed up again a second later, and the color in his cheeks fell away, at the wail of an echoing siren. The sound was distant, though, and became more so after a moment.

"You are safe here," Seven assured.

"I know." Kirill sat back and pulled his knees up, a tall, lean-muscled young man suddenly become a boy.

Seven got up and reached for the television remote control. "Why don't you find us something to watch while I make us some food. All right?"

Kirill took the remote and nodded, haltingly. He clicked past the news reports, to a slow-moving film about provincial village life from the last century. Seven had seen it years before, on base during his army training, so he went to the kitchenette to pull together a mishmash of edibles from the available leftovers. When he returned to the sofa, Kirill lay on his side staring at the screen. He stayed that way until he dozed off a half-hour later, the movie still running and his supper mostly uneaten.

Seven turned off the television and cleaned up the dishes. He pulled out an extra blanket from the closet and laid it over Kirill.

With his charge safe and asleep, Seven retired to his room. He walked into the en suite and stopped at the mirror over the sink, where he peeled off the protective gauze on his forehead to peer at the two delicate butterfly bandages closing the cut above his dead eye. The flesh felt tender under his touch but didn't hurt.

He splashed some cool water on his face and gazed at his reflection – with its square-set jaw and broad brow, the pale scar cutting over his left eye and cheek, and that silver *VII* pin shining at him from his collar, a reminder of who he was supposed to be – and sighed.

Sometimes, a man could not help whom he loved, indeed.

Chapter 6

T HE COMPLEX WAS still in lockdown in the morning. Number Two collected closed-room statements from each member of the teams and staff one by one, leaving everyone else to find other ways to pass the time.

The men's team took over the hotel pool. While not regulation size, it was large enough for them to swim laps, which was what they usually did, anyway. Without the pool, the women's team occupied the workout room, with its weights, mats, and exercise machines. Kirill had already given his statement, so Seven took a run around the hotel perimeter. On his third lap, he saw Number Twelve smoking a cigarette at the rear entrance.

Seven jogged up in a half-sweat and nodded in the general direction of the pool beyond the doors. "I thought you were watching them?"

Twelve grunted in disinterest. He'd been Number Six for a brief spell in his career, but his lackadaisical indifference to the demands of his assignments had gotten him demoted so many times, he'd become a joke. He didn't seem to care, though, about his diminishing importance or anything else. "They're not going any-where," he said around a billowing puff.

Seven made a point to stay upwind of the carcino-genic cloud. "You do remember we are on security lock-down?"

Twelve blew a wet scoff through his teeth. "Metro-politan faggots and coloreds making noise."

Seven stopped his stationary jogging and looked at him a long time before he spoke. "When they are de-ported and shot at for no reason, people tend to be-come angry."

"That's politics," Twelve said, waving his smoking hand. "This is sport."

Thoughts of his meeting at headquarters buzzed in Seven's head. "Number One would say they are the same."

Twelve returned his cigarette to his white-rimmed lips. "One can kiss my wrinkled ass."

That wasn't a pleasant image.

Seven glanced at his watch. "It is almost lunch," he said, partly as dutiful prod but mostly as excuse to get away.

"I'm not keeping you," Twelve said, shallowing his cheeks around another puff.

Seven gave a curt shake of his head but moved inside without further criticism. Number Twelve had done his job his way for decades; there was little chance of him changing, now, especially for a lesser agent's ideals.

He used the pool showers instead of going all the way back to the suite and changed into a clean suit before heading to the pool area. Half of the team was lounging around the edge, while the other half cut through the water in regular beats. Kirill set a steady pace in the far lane, as he usually did, and Seven watched him finish a lap. Youth made the swimmer fast and strong like his fellows, but the drive to be a champion kept him diligent.

Kirill broke the surface at the edge of the pool, spitting water as he raised his goggles and guessed, "Lunch?"

"When you are ready," Seven said.

"I'm always ready to eat!" Kirill said, and hauled himself out of the pool with a single powerful lunge.

Seven smiled; it was good to see that the previous day's events hadn't affected Kirill too much.

They walked over to the showers, with Seven following Kirill at a respectable distance. He readied the swimmer's towel and clothes as Kirill dried off and dressed without pause or blush.

"Should we wait for the others?" Seven asked.

Kirill shook his head as he rubbed the towel one last time over his hair. "No." He snickered and tossed the towel away. "I want first dibs."

Seven chuckled with him as they walked out to the main corridor, toward the commissary. On the way, they went through the hall with the office rooms Number Two had set aside for his interrogations. One of the doors flew open, and Darya came storming out in her playsuit uniform, with Number Fourteen, the women's bodyguard, hustling after her.

Lucky Fourteen, they called her, because she was anything but. While she ranked thirteenth in seniority, superstition prevented the division from having a Number Thirteen. She'd also been a strikingly handsome woman, once. But a fire in the line of duty had melted the skin from her right ear down her neck and – he'd been told – over her torso and most of her arm. She wore long sleeves and gloves and high collars exclusively. Seven guessed she lived most of her hours in a lingering pain. It evoked no sympathy in him, though, simply because she gave no sympathy herself.

"Darya!" Fourteen scolded.

The diver whirled, her ponytail swinging around like a whip. "They cannot do this!"

Fourteen's gaze caught Seven's. The sharp lines of her jaw exuded authority and she hissed to Darya, "Quiet!"

"No!" Darya jut out her chin. "We've done nothing wrong. They cannot simply lock us in here like criminals!"

"Number Two wants—"

"'Number Two wants,'" Darya mimicked with a sneer. She swung her arm toward the debriefing room. "The only thing that little toad wants is power. But *we* have the power," she said, beating her breast. "Without us, he is nothing." She snorted. "I would not be surprised if he set off that bomb himself, just to look important."

Seven's stomach plummeted as he saw Fourteen clench her fist. "No!" he bellowed, but the cruel *pop* of Fourteen's knuckles against Darya's cheek sent the diver's ponytail flying again as she rolled with the hit.

Seven rushed up and snatched Fourteen's wrist in the air. "You should not have done that!"

"Let go of me," Fourteen rumbled.

Kirill came up between Fourteen and Darya. "Are you all right?" he asked the girl.

Darya stood mostly straight, her cheek red and her eyes watering. Her voice, though, came out clear and defiant as she glared hard at Fourteen. "I have survived worse than you."

"You see?" Fourteen said with smug satisfaction. "My discipline makes her strong."

"Your bullying makes me sick," Seven growled.

Kirill bent his head to Darya. "Do you want some ice?" he asked.

She shoved him away, shouting, "No, I don't want *ice*!" before storming down the hall to the lobby.

"Make sure she is all right," Seven said, though Kirill was already jogging on the diver's heels.

Fourteen yanked on her wrist. "She cannot leave."

Seven kept his grip firm. "There is nowhere she can go. And she should not be with you," he added with a snarl.

Fourteen replied with an equal grimace. "I know how to handle her."

"Hitting is not handling!" Seven's boom bordered on a shout, but he succeeded in restraining himself. "We are sworn to keep them from harm. Both out there and in here. You will answer for your actions."

"I get results," she spat up at him. "Number Two sees that."

"He will also learn how you abuse your responsibility."

She snorted a brief humph. "Coddling your ward makes him brittle." She raised her chin. "Mine will be winners worthy of the title."

"Not under your supervision," Seven told her as he released her wrist. He backed up toward the lobby but kept his eyes on her. "Leave Darya be! I will not warn you again."

"I pity your weakness," Fourteen said, turning away.

Seven wasted no more time on her. He hurried to the main lobby, where he found Kirill just outside the doors, his arms hanging at his sides as he watched Darya kick and scream at the bumper of one of the transport vans. Seven let her vent; it would help calm her faster than any pacifying words. Inevitably, her violent kicks died to a weak shove of her heel, and her shouting withered to a series of wheezing puffs. At last, she wilted like a flower deprived of light and slumped onto the offended bumper with her head in her hands.

Kirill walked over and sat beside her. He spoke softly, too softly for Seven to hear, but whatever he said, it made Darya raise her head and start talking in equal quiet. She wiped her face with her hand and shook her head at something. Kirill glanced Seven's way, then tilted his own head as he stood up. He opened his hand. Darya didn't take it but she did stand up with him, and the two of them came Seven's way.

"Are you all right?" Seven asked.

Darya nodded stiffly, and Kirill said:

"Can we stay upstairs a while?"

"I do not want the others to see," Darya murmured.

Seven nodded back at them. He passed Kirill the security card, and Kirill passed it to Darya.

"Go up," Kirill said. "I will bring you some lunch."

Darya stared at the card a moment, then raised her blue-and-gray eyes to look at Kirill. Finally, she smiled a tight, tiny smile and accepted the offer. "Thank you."

Kirill smiled, too. "Blini?"

Darya pressed her lips together again, this time sheepishly. "With chocolate sauce?"

"Okay," Kirill said, and Seven felt a swell of silent pride for him.

They walked to the lifts, and Kirill urged Darya inside the first car. Seven urged him the same.

"Stay together," he told the athletes. "Do not stop for anyone. I will bring lunch up shortly."

"Are you sure?" Kirill said, even as the lift doors began to close.

Seven nodded. "Yes."

Once the elevator was on its way, Seven stalked back up the corridor. Not to the commissary, but to Two's interrogation office.

He shoved the door open, crashing it against the wall. "You need to relieve Number Fourteen," he said without preamble.

Two's initial shock at Seven's entrance became a composed indifference. "Do I?"

Seven crossed to the table, where he dropped both hands in a slap. "Less than twenty minutes ago, I saw her abuse one of the athletes."

Two raised a brow. "You saw?"

"With my own eyes."

Two clasped his hands in front of him and hummed. "I take it from your tone that you will not agree to *un*seeing that?"

Seven drew back from him with a gape. "You knew she was violent. And you did nothing?"

"We were willing to overlook some misconduct, in light of her results. But with a witness...!" Two shook his egg-like head. Seven had a flash of violent thought, of grabbing Two's skull and slamming it against the wall with shattering force. He made no move, though, and the older agent remained unfazed by his own confession.

"I suppose she will have to be reassigned," Two said, and sniffed. "Pity."

"That is all you are going to say?" Seven started to snarl. "Darya was hurt!"

"Miss Vikhrova is insolent and temperamental. Whatever she got, I am sure she deserved."

Seven stared at him. "You care nothing for them, do you? They are mere pawns to you, just a path to the winners' circle—"

"Did you not understand anything that Number One told you?" Two's complexion burned red, the lines around his eyes, nose, and mouth digging deep. "This is not about some ridiculous sports competition! This is about reclaiming our rightful place at the top of the world. Wealthy, powerful men and women will pay – happily! – for our champions. But not if they speak with impudence or devalue their worth with easy-come whores."

Seven felt his stomach cringe, and his voice, when it came, wavered in his ears. "What are you saying?"

"I am saying we already have marriage bids for both Morozov and Vikhrova. All they have to do is win. And all *you* have to do," Two told him with a sharp jab of his finger, "is keep your mouth shut and do your job."

Seven nearly staggered. "You cannot be serious."

Two didn't seem to notice. "Wars aren't won on the battlefield anymore," he said, his voice full of quiet menace. "They are won in boardrooms and on screens, with money and prestige. There is no place for the weak and ugly in this world. Only champions, winners, like the ones we have cultivated here at this facility." He stood up and headed to the door, moving around Seven as if he were no more than a piece of the room. "Now, if you will excuse me, I need to find a suitable replacement for Number Fourteen." He shot a disparaging look from over his shoulder. "Because some people do not know when to look away."

In the devil's wake, Seven clenched his fist. But then he remembered his duty and walked double-time to the commissary. The smells from the trays and plates attacked his senses, making him woozy, but his resolve remained firm.

When he arrived at the suite, his stomach was roiling, and a sticking sweat had started under his arms. He must have looked peaked, too, because when Kirill opened the door for him, the younger man's face lost its smile of greeting.

"Has something happened?" Kirill asked.

Seven steeled himself, stepped inside, and pulled out his earpiece. "Not yet," he said. "Not if I can help it."

Chapter 7

'T HAT CAN'T BE true." Kirill squinted at Seven, the blini in his hand now forgotten. "Can it?"

"Of course, it can," Darya said. The cubes of meat from her kebab lay mostly uneaten in front of her; she hadn't touched them since Seven had told them the darker truths behind their training and sponsorship. "Quit being so naïve."

Kirill frowned. "I'm not—"

"They don't care about us," Darya persisted. "All they care about is what they can get for us." She scowled and pushed her plate away. "I feel sick."

Kirill's gaze strayed to the carpet. "What will we do?"

Darya gaped at him. "We get out of here! That's what we do."

Kirill faced her. "What about the Games? Both of us are sure to place in the final teams—"

"I do not believe this!" Darya thrust herself up from the sofa with a flap of her arms. "You are willing to wait around for them to auction us off, like cattle, just so you can show off how fast you are?"

"That is not what I mean!" Kirill jumped up, too, to stand over her. They stared at each other a moment in silence, then he relaxed his posture with a calmer breath. "If we win, we have leverage," he began.

"And if we lose, we have nothing!" Darya snapped. "And then who knows what they will do to us."

That brought a pause to their arguing. Kirill turned to Seven; Darya did the same. Seven looked from one to the other, caught between fears of both. At last, he managed a statement. It might not allay those fears any, but he knew his job well.

"The Games come with their own risks," he said, mostly to Kirill. "They will get you out of the country, but security precautions all over will be very high, much more than they are here."

"So we have to get out before then," Darya decided.

Kirill swung his stare back to her. "Are we seriously talking about leaving our home? Our families?"

"We are talking about *freedom*," Darya said, and Kirill balked at her.

"As fugitives!"

Darya raised her chin and set her fists tight at her sides. "Not if we go now. Not if we owe them nothing."

Kirill waved his arm over the room. "Except for all of this!"

"Are you afraid?" Darya challenged.

"No," Kirill said, but his gaze shimmered with uncertainty.

Darya narrowed her eyes. "There is no compromise, Kirill. There is slavery, or there is freedom. I know which I choose. You need to decide which you will live with." She spun to the first bedroom and slammed the door after her with enough force to rattle the frame.

Kirill waved a helpless hand. "That is my room," he said, blowing a breath through his cheeks as he landed wearily on the sofa. He looked at his plate but didn't reach for any food.

Seven bowed his head. "Do not feel shame for being afraid. This is not a decision to be made lightly."

Kirill kept staring at his plate. "Darya wants to get away," he muttered. "She has always been ready for this."

Seven moved his hand to Kirill's shoulder. "It is impossible to predict what we will do in any situation until it arises." He gripped the firm, muscled shoulder with sympathy and encouragement. "But your head and your heart have served you well up to now. Trust them, and you will be ready for this, too."

For minutes, Kirill neither spoke nor moved. Then he pressed his lips together, furrowed his brow, and said, "I want to live my own life. I do not want someone else to decide what I will do, or where I will live, or who I will marry." His voice came out in the same deep tone as the night before, but it trembled, too, as if trying to hold up an impossible weight. He looked around the suite, the emotions on his face in conflict with each other. "But my mama and papa gave up everything to send me here. They believed in me. They believed I could be a champion." He turned to Seven, his gaze wavering. "How can I betray them like this?"

Seven laid his hand on Kirill's back. "Your mama and papa made their sacrifices out of love for you. I do not think they would see any choice you make as a betrayal of that love."

Kirill turned to him, and a clarity came to his eyes. "Come with us," he said. "I want you to be free, too. Free to live the life you want, to love the people you choose."

A fierce pounding started in Seven's chest, constricting his throat and pumping the oxygen from his brain. He held his breath to recover himself, then forced the answer from his lips, a simple, croaking, "Yes."

Kirill's smile was tender and sad; Seven nearly drew him into his arms for it. The timid squeak of the bedroom door stopped him, though. They both looked to it, and to Darya standing there in the opening.

"I wanted something more to eat," she mumbled.

Kirill rose from the sofa and crossed to her. "You are right," he said. "We deserve a better future than the one they have planned for us. We will go, together."

"Yes?" Darya said, though her smile was already coming through.

"Yes," Kirill echoed.

Darya's gaze flashed to Seven. "How soon?" she asked, as if he had an answer.

Kirill turned back to him, too, and said, "We will have to be careful, yes?"

Seven tried to stand with confidence, because they seemed to need that, but had to rub his hands on his trouser legs to dry his palms.

"There are too many eyes during lockdown," he said, thinking aloud. "We need to wait until it is over, and things are back to normal. That should only take another day or two."

"And then?" Darya pressed.

Seven kept his gaze steady. "Things go back to normal." He took them in a guarded look. "Train, sleep, eat as you would normally do. But keep your eyes and ears open."

Kirill's expression was blank, but Darya pulled a face.

"That's it?" she said.

"The less you know," Seven said, "the safer you will be. Let me take the risks, for now. It is my job," he added with a tight smile.

Kirill and Darya came to agreement at the same time, nodding together at Seven. He nodded back...even though he didn't have the first clue how to accomplish this new part of a job that was becoming ever more complicated by the moment.

Chapter 8

AS WITH MANY of the tumultuous times through-out Seven's life, Natalya turned out to be his savior.

"Emigration in itself should not be so difficult," she explained as they sat on a bench in the park with their takeaway coffees.

Sitting beside her with his elbows on his thighs, Seven rolled his emptied cup in his hands. He'd had to wait two days for the security lockdown at the hotel to be lifted, another two days for the athletes' commute schedule to the gym complex to return to normal, and an additional three days after that before he felt safe enough to get away for a few hours into the city, under the guise of buying some gourmet chocolates. That excuse might have seemed flimsy if Kirill weren't making an honest effort to be nice to Darya, who did love chocolate.

"Even for who they are?" he asked, and Natalya made a noise of indifference.

"It's a free country. For the most part. Your superiors would probably have more anxiety over any bad press they might get for keeping them locked up, rather than letting them go." She smirked. "Pretty faces always generate more interest for the media."

He marveled at her calm composure and reasoning, when a puzzle piece of her life as he knew it snapped into place. "You have done this before."

She cast him a sly, sidelong glance. "I'm sure I don't know what you are talking about."

Seven swung his head. "Why did I not see it earlier?"

"Because men often do not see what is right in front of their faces," she said, primly but with a touch of annoyance. She paused, then added in a more serious tone, "Unfortunately, even a blind man would spot you running for the border."

He sat up and waved his hand. "I am the lesser concern."

"Not to me," she said, and he exhaled a sigh through his nose.

"Natalya...!"

Her chin puckered with a frown. "There was a time you would call me Tasha."

He coughed. "When we were children!"

The bench creaked as she shifted her hips. "I was no child."

"You were not built like a child," he admitted. "But you were, what? Fifteen?"

"Sixteen," she corrected, before drifting into a thoughtful muse. "And you were that shining young soldier. So proud in your uniform, so tall and strong and beautiful." She smiled in her musing. "Everyone thought so."

"They thought that about you," he said, recalling how she glided with him across that ballroom floor, "in that pink-gold dress that caught the light whenever you moved." He lingered in that far-off memory of simpler, more trusting times, when he'd believed so much in the world around him that he'd been willing to risk his life to preserve it. Now, he was risking his life to run from it.

Natalya lost some of her nostalgia, too. "That dress was hideous," she said, and Seven laughed out loud to spite his melancholy.

"But you wore it like a princess," he said.

One corner of her mouth twitched into a sardonic almost-smile. Then, she became wholly serious once more. "The paperwork I can help arrange. And, it is safe behind embassy walls, relatively speaking. The tricky part will be getting there."

Seven hummed. "We will need a car. Preferably an untraceable one."

"What about one with diplomatic plates?" she said, and when he widened his eyes at her, she raised her unadorned fingers for a blasé waggle. "You are already going to the consulate. It will be easier to get you there in one of their cars."

He didn't quite want to believe it could be so simple. "You think that will work?"

"I have told you: My ambassador friend likes me owing him."

"As much as I owe you?" he asked without jest.

"You owe me nothing." There seemed to be more behind that sentiment, but she didn't articulate it. Instead, she stood up, rattling her takeaway cup. "Give me a few days to make arrangements. And do not call, not on your phone. I will contact you at the hotel."

"How?" he said, rising with her.

"You'll know. Now, come." She used her head to gesture toward the street. "I will buy you those chocolates you need."

He snickered to chide. "I can buy my own chocolates."

"I'm sure you can." Her lips glistened in another wide smile. "But then how would I excuse spending more time with you?"

"Perhaps I am your day-off man. The one you do not need to impress."

"I expend much effort to impress you," she said around a lazy sneer. "You just don't notice."

"I notice," he said in a softer tone, shifting so they faced each other head-on. She was close enough to take in his arms, but he kept his hands at his sides and bowed his head for a hushed confession. "I will miss you."

"No, you won't." Before he could protest, she told him, "I am going with you."

His spine went shock-straight. "What? But your life here—"

"Would not be much of a life," she replied, "if I am going to spend most of it worrying about where you are and what you are up to."

A mix of conflicting emotions rolled in his chest. Despite them, Seven pulled a cautious smile. "Are you sure?"

She put her hand on his sleeve, not gripping but with intent. "I am not going to let you simply walk out of my life again. I have learned my lesson from the last time."

He touched her fingers and let a fuller smile come through. "What would I do without you?"

She matched his smile, though hers broke a bit at the corners. "Let's not find out," she said, threading her hand under his elbow to hold herself close to his side.

Two days later, Seven received a message that there was a package waiting for him at the main desk. He went to retrieve it, only to run into Number Nine on the way.

She didn't look happy. Of course, happiness seemed to be outside the realm of possibility for her, but this was different. She strode toward him on an unerring course, stopping only after she'd successfully barred his way.

"Your target," she said without greeting, and Seven pushed his shoulders back.

"I have told you before—"

"Assignment, then," she corrected, and spread her feet and clasped her hands behind her back, a soldier at ease even though she looked just as rigid as before.

Seven took her stance at face value. "What about him?"

"Tell him to stay away from Darya," she said.

Seven's belly contracted. He'd warned both Kirill and Darya to keep a low profile. If Control decided to put them under extra surveillance – or, worse, under another lockdown – even the plans they hadn't yet made would turn to shit. His brain was racing for an excuse when Nine caught him off his guard once again.

"She's difficult to keep in line as it is, without him arousing her at every turn."

The tension fluttered out from him with three quick blinks. "He *arouses* her?"

"He struts in front of her in his tight clothes and tiny swimsuits. What would you call it?"

"At most, a distraction."

"And how does that help? They're here to train, not engage in extra-curricular hanky-panky."

"Hanky-panky?" Seven repeated, clamping a smile behind his lips.

"Laugh all you want," Nine said, her nostrils flaring ever so slightly. "I take my job seriously."

"As do I!"

"Really?" She raised her chin in sharp defiance. "Tell me: how hard did you have to work to get to Number Seven?"

He drew his brows together. "I don't see what that has to do with anything."

She snorted but gave no deeper reason for that accusation. "I'm the highest-ranking woman in this division," she said through her teeth. "Yet, I'm still only Number *Nine*. If you think I'm going to jeopardize my standing simply because your assignment likes swinging his dick around in front of mine, you are gravely mistaken!"

Seven put a hand up to settle her ire. "I will make sure Kirill keeps the strutting to a minimum," he said, and paused for a smirk. "For everyone's sake."

Nine's only reaction to his teasing was to pull her lips tight before walking away with her spine as straight as a rifle barrel.

Seven allowed himself a breath of relief at her back. In many ways, he preferred Nine to her predecessor. Still, she was a career agent, and ambitious. And, she had those eagle eyes. They would have to be cautious.

He got to the front desk and requested his parcel from the attendant, a dark man with an impressive pompadour that Kirill would have envied. After a quick trip to the back, he laid a long, flat box on the counter. Seven signed for it, thanked him, and carried the box away in his arms, puzzling over its possible contents.

The return address was from a clothier in the city. Seven had passed the storefront many times but had never ventured inside; his salary didn't cover that level of extravagance. Natalya's must have done, though. He couldn't think of anyone else from whom the package could have come.

He took the box to the lockers, where Kirill and the rest of the team were doing an afternoon speed session. They weren't finished, yet, so Seven took the time to investigate the box. He snapped the courier security wrapping with a forceful but controlled pull of his fingers, unraveled a second layer of packaging, and lifted the top of the box.

The white crepe paper crinkled as he slipped his hand beneath it and shifted it aside. Within, a black silk shirt shined up at him. At first, he thought it must be for Kirill, but as he lifted the shirt from the box, he saw that the shoulders were too wide, and the cut of the neck too thick. This was meant for him.

Cufflinks clattered to the bottom of the box, as well as something lighter. He picked up the fallen business card. On one side was embossed the word *Escape*, the name of a dance house in the club sector, while on the other was a handwritten message in a precise, flowing script.

Tomorrow, 9. Bring your friends.

Ever yours,

Cleo

Despite Natalya's sultry subterfuge, a nugget of nervousness jumped from the pit of Seven's belly to the top of his chest. Tomorrow night. The end of his life as he'd known it. So far.

He put the card in his pocket and folded the shirt back into its box, looking up again just in time to see Kirill emerge from the showers in his usual fashion, naked and wet. Seven stood up, grabbed a towel from the pile, and handed it over. He held on to his end for an extra moment, to draw the younger man's attention.

"You have been cooped up too long. We should get out." He paused, and added in a deeper voice, "Tomorrow night."

Panic flashed in Kirill's eyes, but he recovered with a blink. He took the towel and forced a shaky smile. "Darya, too?"

Seven nodded.

Kirill swallowed, put on another nervous smile, and nodded back.

With no time for elaborate planning, they made none, just agreed to get to the club on time the following evening, ready to run.

"We should invite the others," Darya murmured to Seven at the dinner-time dessert table; group meals were the least conspicuous way for them to talk.

He hovered beside her, making a show of trying to decide between pastry or fruit for his empty plate. "Nine will be there, too, then," he warned.

Darya slathered chocolate sauce around a dainty biscuit. "She would be, anyway. It will be easier to slip away if she has more than me to look after, no?"

That made sense, but... "I still do not like it."

Darya brought her thumb, which was marked with a dab of spilled chocolate, to her lips. "What choice do we have?" she said, sucking the chocolate sauce from her finger as she moved away.

Seven had no good answer to that question.

The suggestion of getting out for some entertainment in the city spread through both teams like flames over dry brush. Nearly every training session, meal, and passing conversation to follow buzzed with plans and schemes to make the night one to remember. Seven was certain it would be so, one way or another.

That evening, while Number Twelve brought around the transport van and the rest of the men's team horsed around near the valet stand outside, Seven stood by Kirill in the lobby. He played absently with his own cuffs, but Kirill fully fidgeted, biting his lip and rubbing at the back of his neck like a nervous groom. Seven was about to advise him to relax, because such conspicuous behavior was bound to get noticed by his teammates or – worse – Nine, but stopped himself when the elevator dinged, and from out the opening doors flowed a chorus of feminine laughter. The cluster of women athletes moved past them with little notice, save for Darya, whose clicking gait paused ever so briefly as she spared them a furtive glance beneath her mascaraed lashes.

Seven met her fleeting gaze, and politely waved her on with the rest of the team. Kirill, though, pulled a breath and followed Darya's form with his eyes. He took a step after her, but bumped into Nine's side as he did so, causing a momentary break in the team's smooth movement as a group.

Kirill muttered a swift apology and hurried to the door with his head down. Nine frowned and followed him in a sure-footed march.

Seven let out a sigh, swore to himself, and got ready to run some interference.

Chapter 9

THE BIG PASSENGER van that set out from the hotel rocked all the way to the city, with one of the men's team passing a little flask around and another leading a foot-stomping chorus from the back row that rattled the vehicle's chassis. Seven ignored their misconduct; the more anyone not-Kirill or not-Darya attracted attention, the better the chances of them being able to slip away unnoticed when the time was right.

As for Kirill, the swimmer sat next to Seven, running his lip between his teeth as he watched Darya in the front. Every jolt of the van made her ponytail bounce, as did every laugh she shared with her seatmate, and every glance she shot back to Kirill. Whenever their eyes met, they shared a tiny smile. Seven chose not to notice it. Unfortunately, Nine wasn't so lenient.

When the van pulled up in front of the club, and the teams rolled off of it like a small tidal wave of raucous voices, flashing jewelry, and clashing outfits, Nine grabbed Seven's sleeve at the bottom of the van stairs.

"I thought you were going to control him."

Seven pushed at her hand. "What are you talking about?"

"Your charge." Nine jerked her head toward the athletes making their way into the club. "He keeps looking at Darya."

"She looks at him, too." Seven shrugged. "I think they like looking at each other."

Nine's brows came together. "I'm not amused."

"No," Seven agreed. "You are paranoid." He affected as disinterested a stance as he could muster. "They are young and have been trapped inside for over a week. Who does it hurt if they slip away for some hanky-panky, hmm?" He didn't wait for an answer, but followed the athletes into the club, hoping that would be the last he'd have to deal with Nine.

He found Kirill inside, waiting at the edge of the dance floor. He was still focused on Darya. In her tight purple dress and swinging her arms and ponytail to the boisterous beat, she naturally pulled a man's attention. But where other men in the club cast her lascivious glances, Kirill watched her in quiet bewilderment.

"You are supposed to be having fun," Seven reminded, only barely keeping himself from shouting. The music offered them some loudness cover, but he still strained to hear his own voice.

"She is better at this than me," Kirill replied, his eyes never leaving Darya.

A pang of sorrow tinged with envy dragged at Seven's heart for that look. But he knew Kirill couldn't help the draw of his affection any more than Seven could his own. He nudged Kirill with his elbow and said, "So, let her lead. I will keep watch for Cleopatra."

Kirill nodded, tried to smile, and eased his way down to the crowded dance floor, where he sidled over to the cluster of familiar female figures. One of the other divers drew him into a gyration, and Darya joined them a moment later, shifting him into the middle of a handsome, bouncing line.

The pounding beat changed to a manic squawk that sent the colored lights overhead swinging. Seven peered out over the crowd left and right, but the flashing lights made it hard to see anything. The dancehall beat made hearing equally tricky. All the better to get lost in, but he was wondering how to find Natalya in all of this when her smooth voice blew up at him:

"Hello there, soldier."

He turned, catching his breath at the top of his throat. She looked like a starlet from the last century, in a flowing, fawn-colored cocktail dress with a plunging V neckline and a wide, cinching belt, and twists of her dark hair coiled around each other into a serpentine crown.

He prepped a snicker, even though his heart was thumping. "You look like Eve ready to tempt Adam all over again."

She chuckled with easy sureness. "How fitting. Free will being the original sin, and all." Her eyes took on a meaningful gleam, and she rose up to his ear. "Are they ready?"

He craned his head down to repeat the pseudo-whisper process. "Anxious, but ready."

They swapped angles again. "Have the children dropped their traceables?"

"One at the hotel," Seven said, thinking of Kirill's phone sitting on the table next to his bed. "The other in a friend's purse."

"And yours?"

He managed a half-smile. "Done as soon as I piss."

"Do it now. Our ride is waiting. I will meet you at the coat-check in ten minutes." Then she moved away, leaving no moment for dissent.

He had none, anyway.

He stepped down into the undulating dance crowd, squeezing his way between jumping, jostling men and women engaged in sweaty, joyous obliviousness. Kirill jerked at his tap, and Darya stopped, too. Seven leaned to Kirill's ear.

"Coat-check table. Five minutes," he said, and resumed his press toward the restrooms across the floor.

There were three others in the men's, but none of them were from the team. Seven shimmied around them to the urinal at the end. A water pipe ran along the wall behind it; a good place to stash his phone. There wasn't much in his bladder but he emptied it even so, putting out his free hand to the pipe as though to steady himself. He left his phone there, flushed, and walked to the sink, ignoring the other men around him. When the last one filtered out, he washed his hands and ripped off a paper towel from the dispenser. Then he removed the *VII* pin from his collar, and the comm from his ear, wrapped them both in the towel, and dropped them into the bin with the rest of the garbage.

Out in the club proper, the dancers still undulated. Seven sidled around the edge of them this time, to the coat-check area inside the entrance. He came to it just behind Kirill and Darya, as Natalya greeted them with a guarded smile.

"No second thoughts, I hope?" Natalya asked, when Seven felt a sudden itch at the back of his neck. He turned on instinct, finding Nine shifting their way.

"No second thoughts about what?" the other agent said, her gaze moving in quick, controlled darts, between Seven and the rest of them. "What's going on here?"

Natalya chuckled. "We were just stepping out for a little drive—"

"I didn't ask you." Nine's focus snapped to Seven. She didn't speak but waited for him to do so.

He could have pulled his sidearm, but there was doubt whether he'd be able to draw on her faster than she could on him. She hadn't done yet, though, which gave him a little bit of hope that they could de-escalate this without any violence.

"Please," Seven said, his throat tight for the words. "Just look away. Just for a moment. Forget you saw us, and this will be over that much more quickly."

Nine narrowed her eyes until the whites nearly disappeared. She rotated her stance sideways, and her hand went to the small of her back. Her voice, when it came, hissed in accusation. "You are asking me to neglect my duty?"

"I am only asking you to turn around. If you say you saw nothing, no one will question your record." Something like a smile touched his lips. "In twenty-four hours, you could be the new Number Seven."

Nine pinched her own lips tight. "And here, I thought you were the one I could trust." Now, she pulled out her pistol, a snub-nosed, standard-issue model that matched the one secured in Seven's holster. She kept the muzzle down but the girl at the coat-check table, who'd been silent and unobtrusive until now, let out a yelp of fear.

"Call the police," Nine ordered her. She glared at the rest of them. "Don't move."

The coat-check girl scurried away, to run for it or to phone the police. Either way, it cut their time short.

Seven turned to Nine full-on, puffing his chest and spreading his shoulders to widen his frame. He looked at her but told the others:

"Go."

Nine's pistol came up, straight at him. "I said, don't move!"

"Don't shoot!" Kirill cried, close enough to Seven's ear to tell him he hadn't retreated and hadn't escaped. "We don't want trouble. We just want to be free!"

"We won't be sold!" Darya shouted, and for the first time, Seven saw confusion flicker in Nine's gaze, making her hesitate.

He slammed his palm hard against her gun wrist. She didn't drop the pistol, but he forced it aside, and snapped his head against her brow. She staggered with a broken shout, clutching her head with one hand. He pulled the pistol from her other and clapped it to the side of her head, making her go down.

"I'm sorry," he said, before spinning to the others with the same order as before. "*Go!*"

He followed as they rushed out, unlocking the magazine from Nine's pistol and yanking it free. He popped the round in the chamber, too, and sent everything clattering into a street drain near a dark sedan idling at the curb.

Natalya skittered to a stop beside the car and pulled open the rear door.

"In, in, in!" Seven said, pushing Darya, Kirill, and Natalya inside. He spared a glance over his shoulder, but he didn't see Nine, Twelve, or any other security. Yet.

He ducked into the car, cramming next to Natalya, and hauled the door closed after him with a heavy slam.

"Alex!" Natalya called. "Time to go!"

A familiar voice – the driver who'd returned them to the hotel a few weeks ago – came from the front. "Yes, ma'am," he said, and the car accelerated at a ready pace, merging them into the chaotic traffic of the city.

Seven kept his gaze out the rear windshield for the first six blocks. No lights or sirens followed, though, and no obvious tails. He faced front with a puff of breath at Natalya, who was still smooshed next to him; Darya sat mostly on Kirill's lap, the pair of them crowded against the other door. Seven apologized and tried scooting against his own door, but his size prevented him from giving them much extra space. He settled for stretching an arm behind Natalya, so at least his shoulder was out of the way.

"Is that it?" Darya asked, leaning across Kirill's chest. "Are we free?"

"Almost," Natalya said, and Darya eased back, frowning. Natalya offered her a placating smile. "It will take a few days for the paperwork—"

"A few *days*?" Darya leaned in again, this time at Seven, and hissed, "You said she could help us!"

"We cannot cross the border without papers or permission," Natalya said, before Seven could reply.

"Can't you just forge us papers?" Darya said, and Natalya laughed.

"What a little felon you are!" She waved her hand. "Don't worry. I have friends in the consulate. They will help us."

Darya's brow stayed crumpled when Natalya shifted and said in a hushed, almost maternal voice:

"We need this to be official. Or they will send us straight back again. You do not want that, do you?"

Kirill gave Darya a squeeze and whispered, "It will be all right. Natalya has always done as she has said. You can trust her."

Darya sat back once more. Kirill pulled her closer, though Seven couldn't tell if it was to comfort her or to simply keep her from snapping at Natalya again. The athletes were quiet for the rest of the drive, Darya watching Natalya and Kirill watching Darya, while Natalya sat back against Seven's supporting arm in a way that felt surprisingly natural.

After several minutes, they pulled up to a three-story brick building that stood dim in the middle of the block, save for the bright light shining down over the front stoop. There, a woman came down the steps to meet them. She moved with smooth and confident grace, and while her dark skin had few wrinkles, her fluffy coif was streaked with white that gleamed in the lamplight.

"Francine!" Natalya called.

Seven opened the door and got out. Natalya spilled out after him, from the car to the other woman's arms, where they greeted each other with a quick embrace.

The woman smiled for Natalya before stepping back. "This way," she urged, with a step and a gesture toward the building's open door. "Quickly."

Still standing at the car, Seven beckoned for the athletes. Darya scooted across the seat to him, bending her head low as she poked it out. Kirill came behind her, and she took his hand to hurry them up the short steps to the door. Seven followed them and joined Natalya past the threshold. Once they were all inside, Francine locked the door behind them with the solid thunk of a deadbolt.

She turned to regard them all in one swoop of her intelligent gaze and smiled more easily. "Welcome."

Kirill swung his gaze around at the high walls adorned with framed black-and-white photographs, several of them of well-known government officials of the past, but he didn't let go of Darya's hand. "Is this the embassy?"

"This is the staff residence," Francine informed them, her smile still warm. "But you're safe here. For our purposes, this is sovereign land; your government has no power here."

Darya pushed ahead. "When will we get our papers?"

"The ambassador will speak with you tomorrow," Francine said, and looked at Natalya again. "He's at a function, tonight, or he'd have met you himself."

Darya's frown betrayed some apprehension, but Kirill nodded and gave his thanks.

Alex returned then, with four bundled duffels, each identified by a tag bearing the first letter of their names.

Seven picked up the bag assigned to him and peered inside. Folded there were fresh clothes, enough for three or four days, and a package stuffed with toiletry items. He looked up at Alex and asked, "How did you...?"

"Not me," Alex said. "Thank Natalya."

Seven turned to her, but she dismissed him with a wave.

"A simple bit of shopping." She lowered her chin at Darya. "I had to guess at your sizes, kitten. Hopefully, nothing is too tight for you." She passed a wink to Kirill then, and said, "Your size, I already knew."

Darya looked at Kirill, too, and yanked her hand from his. Kirill froze dumbly, leaving Seven to defuse the moment with an obtrusive chuckle.

"Luckily," Seven said, while plucking at the buttons of his dress shirt, "you know mine, as well."

"Big and tall." Natalya pulled one of her Cheshire Cat smiles. "The way I like."

Francine blew a tiny "heh" under her breath before gesturing them further into the house. "This way," she said.

The vestibule, built beside an octagonal parlor with far too many windows to be secure, opened onto another room with a wide, curving staircase that rose to the upper floors. A swinging door next to it led to what Seven assumed was a kitchen, but they didn't go there, instead climbing the stairs to the second floor. Francine escorted them down a corridor with branching rooms – a smaller, second-floor parlor built above the one below, a closed door that looked like it belonged to a study or bedroom, a similar door down half the length of the corridor, and an open door to a shower bath – to the next staircase. They climbed that one to the third floor, where all the doors stood open to the eye: another full bath, and three bedrooms made up for guests. Natalya walked into the largest of these, tossing her duffel onto a wide-cushioned chair set near the queen-sized bed.

"Well," she said, looking around the room. "It looks like two of us are sharing. Is that all right with you, Dashenka?"

Still standing in the corridor, Darya pulled her chin to her chest and declared, "I am not sharing anything with you!" She turned and stomped away. A moment after, they heard the swing of a door followed by the loud clack of a lock.

Kirill faced the others in the abrupt silence. "I'm sorry," he said in a hushed voice. "She does not mean to be rude."

"It's a lot to deal with," Francine said.

"She is frightened." Kirill swallowed and glanced at the floor. "So am I."

Natalya offered him a look of fond sympathy. "The worst is behind you."

Francine nodded. "Things should be clearer after a good night's sleep."

A solid rest seemed like a lot to expect under the circumstances, but Seven agreed.

"Thank you," he said to Francine, though the words felt insufficient and trite. Nevertheless, their hosts told them to help themselves to whatever they needed, said goodnight, and went down the steps to leave them to their peace.

Once they were gone, Natalya let out a halfhearted chuckle. "Well," she said, exhaling the word around an uneven smile. "I don't suppose either of you gentlemen would care for a nightcap?"

"I think I have had enough excitement for one evening," Kirill muttered.

Natalya sniffed but said no more about that. "You boys want to share the big bed?" she asked, but Seven shook his head.

Kirill had the same answer. "No."

"Are you sure?" she asked, and Seven smiled.

"A gentleman does not make a lady move." He gestured to the corridor. "Kirill, you take the other room. I will take the chair."

"I couldn't—" Kirill began.

"You need your rest," Seven said, preempting any argument. "And, I do not sleep well in a strange place."

Kirill gripped his bag by the handle and paused at the door. "Thank you," he said, to both of them.

Natalya smiled softly. "Sleep well, sweet prince."

As soon as he heard the click of Kirill's door, Seven sighed and turned to Natalya. "Were you serious about that nightcap?"

She dipped her hand into her plunging cleavage, pulled a tiny bottle from somewhere within, and snickered. "Only if you are willing to share."

She passed him the bottle, and he lowered himself onto the edge of the bed for a sip of burning whisky while Natalya toed off her heels and peeled off her stockings. He watched her, soothed by the graceful flow of her hands. The flutter of her stockings joined the dance, and then the slippery flap of her dress's belt.

Seven cleared his throat, unaware he'd been staring. He turned to the wall. "Sorry."

Natalya clicked her tongue. "You know I'm not modest."

He focused on the joint of ceiling and wall, where one could tell the paint colors were slightly different, and kept talking; talking helped him not to think too deeply. "But what about your mystery?"

"I would have that even naked, with you."

"True." He took another delightfully warming sip and kept his eyes on the wall. "I suppose I am the modest one."

"As I have long suspected." Her weight made the mattress shift, and he looked at her again. She'd pulled her dark hair free of its twisted wrap, but spirals of it still clung to their molded shape, creating a riot of glossy whorls around her face. She'd replaced her provocative cocktail dress with a more conservative sleeping shift that covered her shoulders, chest, and hips. Her legs were bare, though, and long and strong as she crossed them one over the other.

Seven blinked, feeling warm and a bit woozy of a sudden.

Natalya brushed close to him. "Let me have a little," she said, when he realized she was asking for the tiny bottle still in his hand. He gave it to her, and she tilted her head back, drinking the whisky as smoothly as if it were water. When she brought the bottle down again, she graced him with a gentle smile, and said, "You were magnificent, tonight."

He shrugged, grateful for the change of subject. "I was doing my job. But, this is not the life you signed up for." He frowned. "I should have kept you safe. And out of this."

She snorted. "I'm sure the blonde bombshell would have liked that."

"She is frightened," Seven said, repeating Kirill.

"She is jealous," Natalya corrected, before shooting him a look of warning. "But do not tell her I said so! She will realize the feeling is mutual."

Seven felt the tickling of a snigger. "You? Jealous of Darya?"

Natalya grunted a distinctly unfeminine harrumph that nevertheless caused Seven to smile. "Have you seen those adorable dimples? To say nothing of the rest of her," she grumbled, and drank again with a shake of her head.

Seven let his gaze wander to her face. "She will never be you," he said, partly to stroke her ego but also because it was true.

Natalya coughed a "heh" of disdain. "And you wonder why I came with you."

She tipped back another sip, probably the last of it, and Seven found himself staring at her again. Her cheek tempted his touch, but he bowed his head and reached instead for her hand resting on the bed.

"I will do my best to protect you," he whispered.

Her lips entered his field of vision; they glistened with a shine of whisky. "I know you will." She pressed a kiss to the back of his cheek, near his ear, and said, "Now, get some rest, soldier. The city might never sleep, but you have to."

He rose away and moved to the chair. Thankfully, she didn't protest; he might not have turned down an offer to sleep in the bed.

He turned the chair to face the door and made himself a cozy space with the blanket and pillow she forced upon him. Once she was finished with the bathroom, he washed up and stripped down, and padded back in his bare feet to the now-dark room. Settling himself into the chair, he listened to the faint sounds of this strange, safe house, and watched the shadows shift across the wall from the lights on the street below, until his body finally overrode the powers of his brain, and he drifted into a deep and weary sleep.

Chapter 10

H E WOKE FROM a lovely dream of bobbing on gently-rolling waves, to a less-lovely crick in his neck and the prod of insistent knocking, and Kirill's whispered voice growing raspier:

"Seven? Seven! Are you awake?"

Seven smacked his eyes open, half-sat up, and groaned, first Kirill's name, then, "What is it?"

The swimmer's tall silhouette broke the light from the corridor. "I'm hungry."

Seven searched for the clock. It sat on the table on the far side of Natalya's bed, where she still slept soundly. The numbers five and twenty-six glowed back at him, and he groaned again. "It is early!"

"I have not had anything to eat since dinner," Kirill pressed. "*Yesterday.*"

"So, go downstairs."

"What if there is no food?"

"This is the staff house," Seven grumbled at him. "I am sure they have toast and coffee, if nothing else."

Kirill paused. "I don't want to get in trouble."

"You won't get in trouble. Francine said to help our-selves. Just try to be quiet." Seven tried to drive home the most important bit: "It is still very early."

"Okay," Kirill mumbled.

The light from the corridor flowed full again. Even so, Seven drifted back into a lightly-uncomfortable doze. He didn't know for how long, when he heard Kirill call for him again:

"Seven?"

Jesus, Seven thought, keeping his eyes closed. "What?"

"How do I make coffee?"

"Wh-!" Seven bolted up, hissing, "You know how to make coffee!"

"There is no machine," Kirill hissed back.

Seven blew a minor blasphemy, tossed off his blanket, and reached for his clothes from the night before. "Fine. Just let me put on some pants."

The kitchen at the end of the first floor hall was not large, but it had a wide sink, a six-burner stove top, and plentiful counter space stretched around the edges. Dark wood cabinets lined the walls and enclosed a tall, well-built refrigerator. A round table stood in the middle, with a centerpiece of recently cut flowers.

Next to the stove, Seven found the coffee press and a bag of beans. He directed Kirill to measure and grind while he set a kettle to boil. A search through three cabinets yielded mugs, plates, and some pans, which inspired Seven to scramble some eggs.

Kirill watched with interest. When Seven was about to crack the first egg, Kirill asked, "Can I try?"

His calmer mood having returned, Seven stepped to one side. "Of course."

Kirill bent his head to crack one egg, then two, being careful not to crush or drip any shell into the bowl. "I need to learn how to take care of myself."

Seven watched him with dutiful interest. "You are more capable than you think."

"What do you think will happen to us?" Kirill asked, his head still down.

"I don't know. This is new for me, too."

"Do you know where they will send us?"

"Hopefully, we will get a choice." Seven recalled the bobbing waves of his dream. "And, hopefully, some-place nice."

Kirill looked up. "Do you think I will still be able to swim?"

"Maybe." His ward's face fell into a frown, so Seven corrected himself, "I am sure you will still be *able* to swim. Though, competition will likely be out of the question, at least for the coming Games."

Kirill returned to breaking eggs. As he started to whisk, he spoke up with more thoughtfulness. "Maybe I can teach other people how to swim. Or help them not to be afraid of the water. Did you know there are actually people like that? Too scared even to dip their toes." He glanced up, meeting Seven's gaze. "Do you think I could do that?"

"I think you could do many things."

Kirill pressed his mouth into a line and resumed whisking. "Not smart things," he mumbled.

Seven held his tongue a moment. "It is not only about being clever."

"Darya is clever."

"Yes. She is also impatient, imprudent, and pig-headed."

Kirill stared at the bowl of frothy eggs in his hand. "That does not make her a bad person."

Seven bit back the smirk that threatened. "Of course not. Everyone is a mix of faults and strengths. Just as you may not be very wily," he said, allowing an affectionate smile to show. "But you are cautious, compassionate, and willing to learn." He gestured to the bowl. "Like this."

Kirill smiled, too. "Can you show me what to do next?" he asked, lifting the bowl, and with a chuckle, Seven started a brief explanation of the combination of butter, burner, and pan. Kirill followed the steps, but paused over the sizzling butter to ask:

"Does Natalya have any bad qualities?"

Seven held in another smirk. "I am sure she would be the first to admit that she is presumptuous, flighty, and domineering. Just as she would likely say that I am dour, judgmental, and too proud to ask for help, even when I need it."

Kirill snickered. "That does sound like you."

Seven took the gibe in stride. "I am old enough to know my own weaknesses. You are still learning."

"I want to be a good man," Kirill declared. "Maybe a husband, or even a father, someday."

Seven chuckled and tapped the pan. "Knowing how to cook helps."

They continued in a comfortable quiet. Kirill had just poured the eggs into the pan when Darya's voice came from the doorway.

"Good morning," she said, and Seven looked up. Kirill did, too, and let out a little gasp. Like Kirill, Darya was dressed in plain track pants and a tee shirt. She'd also chopped off her ponytail, leaving her with a shaggy blonde mop of hair that made her look not unlike a child's doll left out in the rain.

"Good morning." Seven left the obvious unsaid and asked, "Did you sleep well?"

Darya padded to the center table – again like Kirill, she walked barefoot – and slumped into a chair. "I kept thinking someone was going to barge in and drag me back home by my hair," she said, and tugged at the edges of her new, mussed mop.

"Is that why you cut it?" Kirill asked.

The look in Darya's eyes resembled the paranoia possessed by young soldiers who'd just come through their first sortie. Seven was about to offer her some words of assurance, when Kirill went on.

"I like it," he said. "I mean, I liked your long hair, too, but...this is very pretty."

Darya's mouth twitched, giving them a glimpse of the dimples Natalya so envied. "Thank you." The dimples dug deeper. "I like yours, too."

Kirill straightened up in surprise. "My hair? I thought you said I spend too much time on it?"

"You do spend too much time on it," Darya said, still smiling. "It looks better a little bit messy."

A grin started creeping across Kirill's face. "Like now?"

Darya shook her head. "No. Right now, it looks like a hedgehog," she said, and Kirill immediately let go of the pan of eggs, flattening both hands against his head. Darya laughed, a high-pitched sound full of mischief and amusement that Seven hadn't heard her make before.

Kirill lowered his hands and harrumphed. "You can make your own breakfast."

"Oh, I am sorry, Kirill," Darya cooed as she approached them. "Please, let me try some?"

Kirill sidled a step to the left without making her wait. He repeated the instructions Seven had given him, but Darya replied that she already knew how to scramble eggs. That started a new round of playful baiting and ripostes, and as Seven watched them, he decided he should add *resilient* to the list of good qualities for them both.

They took their breakfasts to the table, where they ate in silence for a few short minutes, until Darya returned to her favorite topic.

"When will we get our papers?"

"The ambassador still has to approve our request," Seven said. "I am guessing that requires some amount of protocol."

Kirill looked between Darya and Seven. "What does that mean?"

"Interviews, most likely. Paperwork, too, I'm sure. With luck, they can expedite." Seven didn't say so, but the longer they stayed in one place, the greater the chance of their being found out.

"I hope we go someplace with water," Darya said. "I would like to be close to the water."

Kirill shared a sympathetic smile with his fellow athlete. "Me, too."

Seven gave them an assuring look. "It is a big country. With lots of opportunities."

"This one was supposed to be, too," Darya said, her tone drifting into accusation.

Kirill set down his fork. "Do you think we will change our names?"

"I suppose you could," Seven said. "But, what is wrong with Kirill?"

The swimmer pulled a face. "It's so ethnic."

"At least you are a man," Darya said with a snort. "All doors are open for you." She slumped forward, setting her chin on her hands. "I will probably have to work in a shop. Or wait tables."

Seven brought his coffee cup to his lips, considering for a moment the novelty of a job that was just a job, the concerns of which he could leave behind once the work day was over. "There is nothing wrong with either of those options."

Darya shot him a sharp look. "I bet your friend makes lots of money." She swung her glare toward Kirill and sneered. "Of course, we all know how."

Kirill straightened up in abrupt offense. "What are you mad at me for?"

"Nothing," Darya grumbled. Any greater argument was interrupted by Francine, who arrived at the kitchen just then. The majordomo admitted to surprise at finding so many of them up and about so early, but she seemed grateful they didn't wait for her to serve. She even complimented Kirill on his eggs. Over coffee, she told them:

"The ambassador will be here soon. I woke Natalya, too, because he'll want to speak with all of you."

Seven rose from the table. "Then we should not dawdle." He offered to clean up the breakfast dishes, but Francine told them she would take care of that and urged them instead to get ready.

The duffel supplied by Natalya had only packable casual wear, so just like the athletes, Seven would spend the day in workout clothes. It was a good choice: Once the ambassador got there, the day's schedule was one of meetings filled with paperwork and questions. So many questions, from vitals data and genealogical background to political standing and military history. They each had to submit to a solo interview, probably to compare their stories independently. Seven had his last, but he also had the most to report, being the only one of them who had more than a one-word answer for the military questions. That led into deeper inquiries about training, sorties, and intelligence. He adhered to the soldierly adage that military intelligence was an oxymoron, which elicited a chuckle from the ambassador, Philip, a handsome, well-built man dressed in the trappings of a suit. Seven placed him somewhere in his mid-fifties for the proliferation of white in his close-cropped hair and the deep lines carved into his long cheeks.

"Why do you want to emigrate?" Philip asked.

"The same reason as the others," Seven said, but Philip shook his head.

"For Natalya, this is little more than a change of permanent address. As for the athletes, they're essentially refugees seeking asylum. I can see the fear in their faces, hear it in their voices." He leaned forward on his elbows, his eyes narrowing in scrutiny. "But your case is different. You're not afraid."

The ambassador's voice and manner held a desire for the truth, so Seven responded with honesty.

"I am angry," he said. "I took an oath to defend and uphold the principles of this country. I followed orders, fought in wars, and carried out assignments to the best of my ability, because I believed in the nation I thought we were." He felt a scowl forming. "But I was blind to the one we had become. A country led by despots and demagogues, men who rose to power for the power, not for the principle. Who call us dogs from behind their locked doors and bulletproof windows, and who would punish us as such should we fall out of line." He shook his head and would have spat, if they were outside and not in a pleasant, well-dressed room. "I am done with it."

Philip drew an audible breath and sat back. "The accusations you've raised against your government are very serious. If what you're saying is true—"

"I cannot speak for anyone else in the security division," Seven said firmly, "but I know what I saw. And what was told to me about the athletes, I have told to you, word for word."

To his credit, Philip didn't squirm. "There's no official stance on neo-eugenics."

"But there is on human trafficking." Seven leaned forward this time. "If your country will not help us, I need to find one that will. Kirill and Darya cannot return to the compound. Not now." He jabbed his finger against the hard tabletop. "And I will put my *life* between them and anyone who tries to take them back!"

Philip raised a calming hand. "No one is sending anyone anywhere. I just want to understand the facts of your situation." He lowered his hand and waited.

Seven eased down, inhaling and exhaling a concerted lungful of cool, dry air. After a minute of centering himself, he said, "I understand you are only doing your job. But I am only doing mine. I pledged to protect

Kirill, and, by association, the people with him. I am sworn to keep them safe." He shook his head. "They are not safe in this country any longer. That is why we have come to you. We want to be safe. We want to be free." He swallowed back the cracking of his voice. "I am begging you—"

Philip's hand came up again, this time for a stop. "That's not necessary. We're not in the habit of turning away people who come to us for help." He sat up, his posture and expression becoming calm, composed. Diplomatic.

"The official process takes time," Philip said. "But I think we have enough grounds to move forward."

Seven sat staring at him when Philip rose, smiled, and extended his hand.

"Welcome," the ambassador said, "to the land from sea to sea."

To spite the weight of their conversation, Seven felt a grin split. He jumped up and grasped Philip's hand with grateful force. "Thank you!"

There were more steps to take, but Seven asked if those could wait so he could share the news with the others, whom he'd left in the parlor on the second floor. When he arrived, though, he found only Natalya sitting on the windowsill. She was dressed in track trousers and a sweater, with a cup of coffee resting beside her knee and the glow of the late afternoon sun hitting her face as she gazed out onto the world outside, like a bored catalog model waiting for her photographer. He considered telling her not to sit in such clear line of sight from the street, but quickly decided it wouldn't make much difference.

She seemed to know he was there even without his announcing himself because she said aloud, "Will you miss it?"

He closed their distance, peering over her shoulder at the streets below. "The city?"

She nodded and hummed.

He shrugged. "Not really. I have never cared much for clubs or crowds."

"What about the old neighborhood?"

"You want me to feel nostalgic for a broken-down boys' home and a burnt-out gym?" he asked, briefly snorting. He shook his head. "No. Home is where my heart is."

Now, she turned to him, her expression curious. "And, where is that?"

"At the moment," he said, spreading his hands, "on the second floor of a foreign consulate building."

"So pragmatic," she said, pulling a tiny scowl. Her gaze swiveled back to the window and she sighed. "I will miss this city. The lights, the art, the shops...!"

"You could always start your own shop," he suggested, and smiled. "New home. New opportunities."

As she turned back to him, her face opened up again, once more lively and bright. "I knew Philip would help us."

"I never should have doubted you."

Natalya didn't scold him. Nor did she shout with joy or jump into his arms. She only smiled and put her arms around his neck for a long, strong hug.

Into her hair he whispered, "I was ready to make a triumphant announcement for the sake of the others. But, since it is just us, all I need to say is, thank you."

"Pah!" She drew away, but he saw the brief shimmer in her eyes before she blinked them clear. "We did this together."

"Where are Kirill and Darya?" he asked, glancing about. "I want them to know."

She nodded toward the sofa. "They played nice there for a while. But, when I asked if they wanted a coffee and our young prince said yes, the little minx apparently took that as me trying to seduce him. In this outfit," she said, blowing a snort as she waved her hand over herself, "if you can imagine."

Seven hummed impartially. "What happened then?"

"She stormed off," Natalya related in a sing-song cadence. "I told him to go after her. That is the last I know."

"Any idea where they may have gone?"

"If he remembers his lessons, they could be in bed by now."

The tightness in Seven's back and neck, which had dissipated with Philip's assurances, abruptly returned. "You are not serious," he said, but Natalya returned a stony face.

"I never joke about romance."

"This morning, they were making fun of each other's hair...!"

"Wildfires can start from an unexpected spark," she said. "It is the nature of passion in the young."

Seven grunted. "I suppose."

"If she is determined to stay angry at him, she will have closed her door in his face." Natalya pressed her lips into a tiny smirk. "And if he is determined to win her back, he will be standing outside of it."

Seven sighed and thanked her, then made his way up to the third floor. He didn't find Kirill standing outside Darya's door, but that was because she hadn't closed it on him. Rather, he heard both their voices coming from inside her room. Their tones were heated but hushed; apparently, he'd come upon them with their argument still rolling.

"You do not understand anything," Darya was saying, her voice like viper's venom.

"Then explain it to me," Kirill hissed in return. "I cannot read your mind! I don't know why you are so angry with me."

"I thought we were doing this together!"

"We are—"

"So why is *she* here?"

"Natalya is helping us."

"Helping *you*," Darya seethed, and even though Seven held himself back so as not to be seen, he could imagine the defiant jut of her chin. "Not me. She could not care less about me."

"She just does not know you."

"Like she knows you? All her intimate knowledge about you. Like the size of your clothes? The size of your cock, maybe!"

"I don't know what you want me to say," Kirill mumbled, and a heavy silence fell between them. Then, Darya's voice, once again hushed.

"Are you in love with her?"

"No," Kirill said without hesitation.

"But you think she is beautiful!"

"So? I think you are beautiful, too."

Darya's voice trembled. "No, you don't."

"Are you crazy? Of course, I do!"

"You never talked to me," Darya countered. "Never came to me. Never got dressed up or fixed your hair for me."

"Because I thought you didn't like me!" Kirill answered. "I thought I had no chance with you. The way you stood up to Number Fourteen," he said, his voice dropping rapidly into a hush. "And how confident you were at the club. You are so much more than any woman I have ever met. Brave, and strong, and clever. And I—!" He didn't finish for a gasp.

Wondering what he'd been about to say, Seven pushed his feet toward the doorway, but stopped short the step that would have brought him fully into sight. For there was Kirill, sitting on the edge of the bed, with Darya arched over him, holding his face for a powerful kiss that occupied them both.

Seven stepped back, nearly flat against the wall, and let out his breath. Another weight he hadn't known he'd been carrying in his chest seemed to lift away.

He retreated to the stairs with a muted, shuffling step, easing himself down one stair, a second, and a third. There, he paused, cleared his throat, and called as though approaching for the first time, "Kirill? Darya?"

"Uh! Just- just a moment," Kirill called back. He appeared in the corridor, straightening his shirt, and glanced into the room. As Darya came to his side, he stammered, "We were- we were just—"

"What did the ambassador say?" Darya asked, and Seven smiled for her quicker composure.

"They will help us," he told them.

Their young faces went blank. Darya murmured, "We are free?"

"Yes," Seven said.

"All of us?" Kirill asked, and Seven nodded.

"Yes."

For a moment, neither athlete moved or made a sound. Then, Kirill broke into a grin spreading wide with joyous relief, and Darya's eyes shone with liberated triumph, and they threw themselves into the other's arms. They started to laugh together, when Kirill let go of Darya and put his arms around Seven.

"Thank you!" Kirill cried, half into Seven's neck.

A warning that this was only the first step came to Seven's tongue, but he didn't say it. Instead, he hugged

Kirill back as he swallowed down the sappy feeling that rushed to the top of his throat.

"My friend," Kirill said with a squeeze of his arms. When he drew back, his eyes were clear, the gold flecks gleaming. "We could not have done this without you."

Seven stepped back, too, letting him go. "I could not have taken this step without you, either."

Kirill's grin flashed again. "We should celebrate! With food, yes?"

"I am starving," Darya agreed.

"Maybe we can make something," Kirill said, and grabbed her hand for a hurried dash down the stairs, leaving Seven to follow after.

Down in the kitchen, Francine was already preparing: platefuls of baked Brussels sprouts beside pierogi stuffed with mushrooms and spinach salad dressed with apple slices. The worries expressed just that morning faded from their awareness, replaced by a zesty anticipation to begin their new lives of freedom and choice. For Kirill and Darya, that apparently included an open desire for each other, at least the way Seven understood their not-so-subtle sways and touches beneath the table. When it was time for coffee, they stayed with the group, but it was obvious their interest lay elsewhere.

After supper, Philip left, and Francine and Alex said goodnight. The rest of them retired to the third floor, where Seven hung by Natalya's door, watching as Kirill did the same by Darya's. The young diver came out, briefly, in a tee shirt and maybe panties, and drew Kirill to her with a whisper and a clutch of his hand. They kissed, oblivious to their location. Then Kirill shuffled them into Darya's room. As the door closed behind them, Seven heard Natalya mutter:

"He is too young for you, anyway."

Seven knew that as he faced her and saw her gentle frown. While touching, her concern was unnecessary, so his reply was wry. "I just hope they are careful."

"They ought to be. I packed them plenty of condoms."

Seven popped his eyes wide. "What?"

She shrugged. "Always be prepared. Isn't that your soldiers' motto?"

"Scouts' motto," he corrected, and sighed. "Do you have any of that whisky left?"

"Sadly, no." Her expression alighted with a tiny smile. "How about gin?"

She meant the card game, not the alcohol, but that was all right. The changing hands provided them with a comfortable cover to talk about less serious subjects while they sat together on the bed. When the cards began to blur in front of his eyes, though, Seven yawned, dropped them to the blankets, and grumbled a curse.

Natalya chuckled for his vulgarity, and said, "Sleep here tonight."

He rubbed his neck. "That chair is not as comfortable as it looks."

She clucked. "I meant here, you big bear. In the bed."

"No...."

"Yes," she said, laying her hand on his arm.

He was about to protest more, but the mattress was wide and long, the downy blanket soft, and the sheets sweet-smelling. And, he was so very tired.

"Are you sure?" he asked.

"Yes," she said again, and showed him her wily smile. "Besides, these walls are not very thick. You don't want to be next door to the stallion and his mare all night."

"You are right," he said with a playful scowl. "I don't."

They shared a lonesome laugh. He settled next to her, on top of the blanket so that a layer separated them; his blanket from the night before, brought from the chair, would serve him well enough. She clicked her tongue at his antiquated propriety but didn't protest more than that. Her head lay nearly on his shoulder, and he noticed it wasn't the sheets that smelled of sweet lilacs, but her.

"See?" she whispered. "Not so bad, is it?"

The weight of his eyelids brought them down, but Seven managed to reply, "You are a good friend."

"Thank you, and you're welcome. Now, hush," she said, "and go to sleep."

He relaxed his back and let the lesser concerns of the day rise out of him. Lying on the bed, he felt as though he were once more being carried away on the gently-lapping waves of his dream, into a great but peaceful new unknown. At the edge of his awareness,

he felt Natalya slip her hand into his, and that was how
he fell asleep.

Chapter 11

A TICKLING IN his nose nudged him awake. Seven opened his eyes to find himself curled against Natalya, with one arm draped over her. His mind dismissed any potential alarm by reminding him that it was chilly, she was warm, and her blanket was still gathered between them. His body, however, ignored those pragmatic excuses and rewarded him with a sizable morning erection.

Natalya stirred and half-turned her head toward him. The motion bunched her hair between their faces, making him pause. It still smelled of lilacs.

He eased away, clamping his teeth in a careful grimace, even as she said:

"Semyon?"

He froze, and whispered, "Go back to sleep."

She hummed a plaintive noise. "It's cold."

"I won't be long. I just need to use the toilet."

She let out another little groan and turned so she was facing him, her expression smoothing quickly from brief annoyance to sleepy contentment.

He slipped out from under one side of his blanket, at the same time drawing the other edge over her.

She snuggled into it with a tiny smile, and he paused again. She looked calm, tender, and very lovely. He very nearly stayed in bed with her, but for the prodding of his bladder.

The early morning chill pricked the soles of his feet as he crept down to the communal bathroom at the end of the hall. Kirill's door stood open; the bed inside sat empty. Farther down, Darya's door was ajar. Seven bent his ear to the gap to listen when the sharp clatter of the coffee grinder startled him from his pointless prying.

After relieving himself, he made his way downstairs to the kitchen, where he found Kirill pouring coffee into two mugs. The coffee looked thin and unappetizing, but Kirill's smile intimated an enviable happiness. Seven took care to wait until he'd finished pouring before he announced himself.

"Lessons learned, I see."

"I thought it would be nice," Kirill said, his smile growing to a grin. "She did some *very* nice things for me last night."

Seven held up his hand. "Please...!"

"Sorry." Kirill waited for a single breath, then asked in a careful and curious voice, "Did you and Natalya do anything nice last night?"

"We played cards," Seven said. "And talked."

Kirill leaned across the counter, his eyes gleaming. "Oh, come on. You can tell me."

"Tell you what?"

"About you and Natalya!"

"What about us?"

"How you are together now."

"What are you even talking about?"

Kirill dropped his voice to a mutter. "You made love last night, didn't you?" he asked, and Seven staggered.

"We did nothing of the sort!"

Kirill straightened up. "But...you were in bed together this morning."

"That does not mean anything!" Seven snapped. "I was only...!" He stopped on a half-breath, thinking abruptly of that comforting, wholesome feeling he'd had when he'd woken next to Natalya. "She asked me," he said, and followed with a hurried further explanation. "To sleep in the bed. But only because it is more comfortable than the chair."

"And there was no other bed available," Kirill said, with a dry sarcasm that was completely new for him.

"That is your bed," Seven said. "I did not know you would not be using it."

Kirill's skepticism remained intact. "Right."

Seven glowered. "You don't believe me?"

"What I don't believe is that you wouldn't know where I am or what I am doing at any given moment of the day or night. So do not use me as an excuse for why you got into bed with Natalya."

"It is not an excuse!" Seven's voice came out strained in an effort to stay hushed, but even he heard the desperation in it. He drew a breath, swallowed, and tried again, this time managing a bit more control. "You know it cannot be that way between me and her."

Kirill's expression turned innocent. "Why not?"

"Because," Seven said, though he halted there for a string of anxious heartbeats. "I have told you about what happened during the war," he managed at last. "About Erik."

"Your nurse? The one you did not tell how you felt? Who you said would probably not even remember you?"

Kirill sounded neither accusatory nor confused. Nevertheless, Seven felt a clutch of shame in his belly.

"A man does not have those feelings for another man for no reason."

"But you did have a reason," Kirill said calmly. "You had been hurt, and he helped you. Just because you felt something for him then does not mean you cannot feel something for someone else now. I have seen the way you look at each other. You love her."

"Not-!" Seven shut his eyes and shook his head. "Not that kind of love."

"Are you sure?"

Seven continued to shake his head, but the memory of Natalya's warm and gentle touch, the sound of her snicker, and the comforting smell of her hair jumbled like loose marbles in his brain, making it hard to think. The shame became pain, but he managed to get out:

"She deserves a man more than me. One who can provide for her needs."

Kirill said nothing for a moment. Then: "A man is more than the sum of his measurements."

Seven looked up to see Kirill's soft smile. He opened his mouth for more rebutting, but no words were ready.

"We cannot help who we love," Kirill said. "Or, how."

Seven coughed up a little smile of his own. "You are starting to sound like Natalya."

"She taught me many things." Kirill lifted his chin and touched his chest, affecting an air of wisdom. "But the most important, she said, is to listen to what your heart tells you." He smiled wider, as he put the mugs and toast onto a large serving dish that functioned as a platter. "Right now, mine tells me to bring this to Darya while I still have the element of surprise," he said, and was out the kitchen door before Seven could say anything more. Not that he wanted to; stopping Kirill would have been just an excuse not to examine his conflicting thoughts.

He picked up his coffee and walked to the windows, peering out at an angle to the yard below, where a street cat rummaged in the rubbish as the light came up over the rooftops. His focus blurred as he sipped his coffee and considered what could come next. Not for Kirill, nor for Natalya, either. But for himself, and the life he could make from here.

For a long time, he'd defined his life by one thing: his job. But life was more than just the job. It was feelings and experiences, memories and relationships, dreams and desires. And love. What did he love?

He loved Kirill, though not in the way he'd first thought. He loved Natalya, too...though, again – possibly, apparently, if he were honest with himself, very likely – not in the way he'd first thought. She was his friend, perhaps the best friend he'd ever had. She trusted him, accepted him, let him be his own man, whomever that was: Number Seven or Semyon, soldier or bodyguard, friend or...what? Which did she want? And, what did he want?

He wanted to go back to bed, back to Natalya. Maybe she'd be awake, and they could talk. Of course, what was the rush? They had plenty of time, now—

A sharp clang of metal resounded through the house, as rapid and loud as machinegun fire rattling against a tank hull. The clatter came again, and Seven's more rational mind recognized it as the knocker on the main door.

He set his cup in the sink and padded to the main hall. Francine was coming down the stairs, tying a dressing gown closed around her waist; Alex peered after her from the middle of the staircase. They gave him silent motions to stay back, but he couldn't help angling himself to see around Francine's arm when she opened the door.

Number Two showed off his oily smile. "We are sorry to disturb you so early, madam," he said. Beside him, Number Fourteen removed her sunglasses and scowled.

The coffee in Seven's belly felt like it curdled at the sight of them. He shifted back with a broken breath at the same moment that Francine attempted some cooler civility.

"May I help you?"

"We've found what we're looking for," Two said, still unctuous. He raised his chin and spoke to Seven. "Our surveillance can pinpoint a beetle on a sand dune at eight hundred yards. How long did you think it would take us to find a fool as big as you, even in a city this size?" He took a step to the threshold, but Francine put out her arm, barring his way.

"I'm sorry," she said. "Do you have a warrant?"

Two held his step but lowered his head. "You are harboring fugitives."

"They're refugees," Francine corrected, and Two scoffed.

"They're enemies of the state! They betrayed their country."

"We betrayed nothing!" Seven said, swooping to Francine's side. He brushed aside her concern, keeping his full attention on the pair of black-suited agents. "You swore to us liberty, opportunity—"

"And you swore an oath," Two hissed.

"To protect," Seven said. "To serve—"

"You serve *us*!" Two's eyes went red and his lips peeled back from his gums. "Now, you bring out those athletes, or we will come in and take them."

"You step one foot into this house," Seven growled, "and I will throw you back out again with my bare hands."

Francine stepped between them. "This is a diplomatic residence," she told Two pointedly. "You have no jurisdiction here. Now, I suggest you leave, unless you want an international incident on your hands."

"We're not going anywhere," Two began, when Fourteen came to his side, head down and shoulders tight.

"Hand over the athletes!" she shouted, pulling her sidearm. "Now!" The gun flew up toward Francine, its metal mouth flashing furiously under the light.

"Fran!" Alex cried. He trundled down the stairs, but Seven was nearer.

He shoved Francine to the side, behind cover of the wall, and snatched for Fourteen's gun. The muzzle barked, and for a second, Seven didn't know where the bullet went. Then a burning pain raced up his arm and he staggered, clutching his bloodied hand in the other.

"*Semyon*!" Natalya screamed from behind him, just as Two hollered:

"You idiot! Stop shooting!"

But Fourteen's gun snapped again, and this time, a flood of deafening silence took the place of Seven's pain and terror.

He lurched in a turn. Natalya came running toward him, but without sound, her voice dissipating upward as he fell to the floor.

The world dimmed.

She pulled him into her arms.

He wished for more time, but there was none.

Chapter 0

A GULL CRIED, sharp but far away. The faint smell of salt tickled the hairs in his nose. He drew a long, chest-filling breath, dragging that air into his lungs.

This wasn't death.

The world felt cool. The gull cried again. A few more long-drawn breaths, and he heard Natalya say:

"Hello again, stranger."

He tilted his head to the sound of her voice and opened his eyes, the lids parting with a sticky click. Slowly, Natalya's face swam into focus. Her hair was pulled back to her crown, with little flyaway wisps at her temples flowing free and touched with smoky-brown highlights that brought out her natural complexion. She had very little makeup on, just a touch of darkness and shine at her eyes and lips. He could make out gentle crow's feet around the former and worry lines around the latter, but as she came close to him, those all seemed to disappear.

His voice came out a croak: "...*hoo-ehrr*?" He tried to loosen the phlegm, and a dry discomfort like the run of sandpaper along the membranes inside his throat made him grimace.

She lifted a cup and pushed a spoon to his lips. "Don't try to speak. The tubes haven't been out for long."

The stuff in the spoon was cold – ice – and, as he sucked on its soothing wetness, she told him:

"You are in hospital. Almost four months, now."

He drew a breath full of ice that made him cough. He tried to lift himself up but couldn't do it, instead falling back against the bed beneath him.

A motor whirred as she raised the bed higher, until he was mostly sitting up.

The lines around her mouth deepened into a frown once more. "You were shot," she said, and he closed his eyes, recalling the sound of the gun, followed by a jumble of images and sensations that had nothing to do with being shot: flashing lights, droning beeps, the wheeze of pumping air.

A stroke of her fingers through his hair made him open his eyes again.

"We thought you were going to die," she went on and smiled faintly. "But you proved all of us wrong." She resumed her slow spooning of ice chips. "There were so many operations, so many tests, so many hours waiting for you to wake up. But through it all, your heart stayed strong. The first time you opened your eyes, you grabbed the nurse by the arm and said, *'beach'*. Do you remember that?"

He shook his head.

She pressed her lips together and passed him another spoonful of chipped ice. "That's all right. They said memory could be difficult. Anyway." She nodded across him and chuckled. "We could not bring your hospital room to the beach, so we brought the beach to you."

He turned his head. On a table next to the bed sat a tiny portable speaker attached to an audio pod, from which the sounds of gulls came. Beside that was a shallow plastic dish filled with seashells, sand, and a few stalks of purplish flowers. Guarding it was a tiny stuffed toy bear with a shirt proclaiming, *Get well soon!*

"Kirill refreshes the flowers every day before he goes to work," Natalya said. "Do you remember him? Our Kiryushenka?"

This time, he nodded.

She snickered. "How could you forget, eh?" She spooned him some more chips. "He and Darya are attached at the hips these days. Philip recommended they apply for the national athletics program, but in the meantime, they work in one of those flashy bars you have always hated. She sells liquor to leering businessmen," she said in a telling-tales voice, "and he brings drinks to slow-thinking party girls. But, they are happy." She pulled a quick face. "They also screw like rabbits. I have envied you this private room these last few months."

He managed a weak smile.

She chuckled again as she offered him another spoonful of ice. "Luckily, they are on the top floor, so you don't really notice it until the ceiling starts creaking."

He swallowed the chips before they'd finished melting. The ice scratched, but he didn't care; he needed to speak. He grasped her hand with the cup – God, he could barely manage it – and rasped, "Thank you."

Her face went blank. Then, her full smile returned. "Hush," she said, tipping another spoon of ice to his lips. "And rest. You need to get better."

It took time to regain his weight, to say nothing of his balance, speech, and strength. But, just like the last time he'd teetered on the brink, he pushed himself through recovery and rehabilitation with the help and encouragement of his friends.

On the day of his discharge from hospital, as he finished dressing into a set of new trousers and shirt to fit his bedrest- and rehab-slimmed frame, he felt ready to begin his new life, when his old one walked through his open hospital room door.

"You look surprisingly fit," Nine said, looking equally fit, herself, in her tailored gray pantsuit.

He froze. "What are you doing here?"

"Relax," she said, in an uncharacteristically blasé drawl. She settled into the chair across from the bed, where Natalya usually sat. She even crossed her legs. "I'm not here on orders, and I'm not out for revenge. I just want to talk."

He took her at her word and shifted his hips on the edge of the bed. "I'm sorry," was the first thing to come to mind. "I did not want to hurt you."

"You stole my gun and hit me with it." Her serious frown returned. "That was...insulting. But I heard your story," she went on before he could make another apology. "And I don't blame you for what you did. Not much, anyway."

He pulled his brows together. "You...heard?"

"News travels fast when it sets things on fire. The inquiry into the events at the embassy shone a bright light on the security division. As it turned out, there was a lot going on in the shadows." Her gaze drifted away a second, only to snap back to him with her typical cool efficiency.

"You know," she murmured, as if trying to keep a secret, "if you'd told me at the start what you were doing, and why, I would have helped you. Not that it matters, now."

Despite a tug of shame, he said, "I could not take that chance."

Her dark eyes bored into him. "Not all of us are interested in preserving the old order. Many want change. Some of us have even started to make it happen." As she tilted her head, he noticed for the first time the new pin on her lapel, with the very familiar letters *VII*.

"Congratulations," he said, nodding at the pin. "You will make a fine Number Seven."

The ghost of a smile touched her lips. "I don't intend to stay Number Seven for long. There's a new wave coming. It's going to wash all the old away. We'll have a better vision, and better leadership." That faint smile became a smirk. "I'm thinking a woman at the helm, for a start."

Now, he started to smile, too. "I can think of a more-than-capable woman to fill that role."

"That woman could use a good man backing her up," she said, but he shook his head.

"That is not my life anymore. Never again, in fact."

The dark gaze held steady for a long minute, like a sphinx's stare. Then she blinked and smiled with one half of her mouth. "If that's your decision." She stood up, straightened her suit jacket, and stepped to the door. She paused there and looked back at him from over her shoulder.

"Stay out of trouble," she said, ending with, "Semyon," before she was gone.

He let out a long, low breath. He'd need to change that name.

Barely a minute later, Natalya walked in, wispy in her casual jeans and cardigan, and completely unaware of the woman who'd stood where she was only a few moments before.

"What are you still doing here?" she said, and humphed in amusement. "Don't tell me you are getting nostalgic for this dreary little room?"

He stood up, as straight and as tall as he could muster, which was a fair bit. "No. No, of course not." He picked up his small bag of personal belongings. "I am happy to leave," he said, and was, especially with her.

Kirill and Darya greeted them in the lobby with enthusiastic cheers that made the other people around glance their way. A few staff members offered them smiles, and Seven smiled back, relieved just to be leaving.

"You look *so* much better," Kirill said as he came in for a strong hug that almost took Seven's breath away.

"Since yesterday?" Seven joked around a grunt.

"Yes," Kirill said emphatically.

"Because you are getting out of here," Darya said, showing off her dimples in a grin.

"And going home," Natalya said in a voice so full of tender hope, Seven heard his own voice crack in return.

"That sounds nice."

It was a long drive along uneventful highway from the hospital to the little municipality on the British Columbia shore, but it was also pleasant to relax in the back seat while Kirill drove. He'd become confident behind the wheel as he and Darya talked about random points of interest. Seven just smiled as he listened and held Natalya's hand.

The rental house provided by Philip's colleagues in the immigration office sat on the outer curve of a residential development. It was small – just two narrow floors with an attic loft – but what it lacked in size it made up for in equal parts privacy and proximity to the markets, shops, and beach. Their fellow residents greeted them with friendly acceptance, too, lending credence to the translation of the municipality's name, "people of the safe harbor."

Seven spent most of his time getting a feel for their new home. He liked stretching his legs every day along the touristy streets, secluded hiking trails, and bustling beach. And he enjoyed being just a regular man, for now, with a regular life and regular friends.

Kirill walked with him most days, and their conversations revolved around plans for both the present and future. He talked a lot about wanting to bring his parents up despite their assurances that life was ever the same as it had been; there didn't seem to be any repercussions against them for his leaving. Perhaps Nine – or whatever Number she was, by this time – had gotten farther with her own plans for administrative change. He was anxious for them to meet Darya, though, with whom he'd grown much more serious over the last few months. They'd even discussed moving farther down the coast to pursue non-competitive careers at the National Park, Darya with the educational team and Kirill with the conservation crew. Swimming and diving could still be part of their dreams there, as well as their reality. Seven wondered if making love on the moonlit beach was part of that, too.

While Kirill usually joined him for his walks during the day, Natalya offered her ready companionship in the evenings. She'd discovered a lucrative lifestyle as a fashion consultant for the municipality's population of wealthy retirees and, while it wasn't escorting prominent Manhattan businessmen and politicians, it more than paid the bills. And, like Kirill and Darya, she seemed happy. So much that Seven felt uncomfortable not being able to contribute beyond some cooking and basic housekeeping.

"Don't be silly!" Natalya told him on one of their twilight walks along the beach. She'd bought them some coffees to sip against the salty breeze, though she left hers mostly forgotten as she held to his arm like a chatty tour guide. "You are still recuperating."

"You heard the doctor," he reminded. "I am one hundred percent!" He shook his foot out of a tangle of weed that had either washed or been dragged up to the sidewalk. Likely the latter; he'd seen more than one laughing child trailing the vines after them like waterlogged kites. "Or, at least, what counted for one hundred percent before."

Natalya made that familiar clicking sound in her cheek. "You have always put others ahead of yourself. It's time to collect on that. Besides," she added after a pause, "I like having a house-husband."

She chuckled, but he drew them to a slow stop. A light silence floated around them on the breeze. They were alone here, separate from the waning cavorting of amusement-seekers on the sand and the burgeoning bustle of restaurant-goers on the street.

"Natalya," he said.

"Semyon," she replied cheekily, though that made him pause. He didn't like that old name. It didn't feel like him anymore. Neither did Seven, of course; Seven was another life left behind. He'd have to get around to putting in that change-of-name request. Simon, maybe; it didn't matter at the moment. He'd left his old life behind. Though, there was a part of that old life that he still wanted. A part he'd never admitted, until now.

He faced her, and said, "I love you."

Her irreverence fell away as she blinked at him.

He kept going. "I would like to be there for you, as you have been there for me. I cannot tell you what that means beyond what I feel in my heart, but, perhaps, I can change who I am—"

"I would not want you to." A shiny film had bloomed across her gaze, which cleared at a blink that set free a spill of tears down her cheeks. She reached up and laid her palm to his face.

"I love the man you are," she said, her thumb stroking the scarred skin beneath his dead eye. "I have always loved the man you are."

Something inside him fluttered and made his breath falter: it went in and came out as a stutter of air. No words could match hers, so he said, simply, "Tasha...!"

She put her arms around his neck and hugged his body close to hers. He did, too, fiercely and briefly. Before they eased out of their clutch, he pressed a kiss to her forehead. Anything more would have felt forced; anything less, not enough.

When they parted, she smiled up at him with a look of deep feeling, her green eyes shining with happiness. She broke into a gentle little laugh. "What do we do now?"

He grasped her fingers loosely but with love, smiled, and told her, "We live."

ABOUT THE AUTHOR

By day, Mayumi Hirtzel works as a video producer and media programmer. In her spare time, she creates worlds and universes populated by wild, eccentric, passionate characters who often ignore their initial plots in favor of a far more complicated one, and who seldom give up even after their stories are supposed to be done.

She lives in Philadelphia, PA, with her family, on land borrowed from a colony of feral cats.

Follow her writing journey at bonusparts.com

www.ingramcontent.com/pod-product-compliance
Lightning Source LLC
Chambersburg PA
CBHW070509200726
48293CB00007B/2455